The Last Surrender

ZONDERVAN HEARTH BOOKS
Available from your Christian Bookseller

A HEARTH ROMANCE

The Last Surrender

Sallie Lee Bell

ZONDERVAN
PUBLISHING HOUSE

OF THE ZONDERVAN CORPORATION   GRAND RAPIDS, MICHIGAN 49506

PREFACE

This novel is a romance portrayed during the time of the War between the States. Every effort has been made to be accurate in every portrayal of happenings during this time.

The incidents which took place during Butler's occupation of New Orleans are true to history and nothing has been exaggerated in the slightest.

Every effort has been made to keep the sentiment which dominates the story from narrow sectional prejudice. At this late date, perhaps those whose forefathers suffered on both sides in this struggle may recognize now how unnecessary the struggle was. There was right and wrong on both sides, but it is hoped that with the passing of the years, all bitterness may now be wiped out in thanksgiving that we live in America, a united nation, where its people enjoy blessings that no other nation is privileged to enjoy.

We all realize now that this might never have been possible if the nation had remained divided. We feel that God's hand was in the struggle, welding a nation, once divided briefly, into a mighty force which can and should be used to bring liberty and release from suffering to others less fortunate than we.

The Last Surrender

1

It was a perfect spring morning, just cool enough to inspire one to activity. Later on the hot summer would come with its enervating influence, but today there was the mere breath of a departing winter to stir the faint breeze which wandered into the room of Diana Wilborn and stirred the ruffles bordering the tester of the four-posted bed.

She lay there for a moment, relaxed and drowsy under the ruffled organdy spread. Then she stretched her slender white arms and yawned lazily. Presently she threw back the cover and slipped her feet into the bedroom slippers beside the bed. She went to the window and stood while she brushed her hair and looked out upon the early spring day.

The sun was already making a pattern of light and shadow upon the long walk leading from the house to the gate. It peeped down through the ancient oaks which bordered the path.

It was good to be back once more in their plantation home, Diana mused, as she began to dress. She loved the old place and the peace and quiet here after the stress and strain of the busy social season in New Orleans. Before long, however, their peace and quiet and relaxation would end. There would be dinners and barbecues, parties indoors or out under the trees, when guests from the city would ride out to enjoy the hospitality at the big house and to escape from the summer heat of the city.

Diana combed her long black hair and fashioned it into a soft knot at the back of her head. Tendrils of inky blackness which accentuated the whiteness of her skin crept forth from the shining mass of her hair and nestled about the lovely oval of her face.

She fastened the tight fitting riding habit of dark green about her slender form. She was tall and graceful in every line and the habit revealed the perfection of her figure. The white ruffles at her throat rested in a cloud beneath the dimple of her chin. She surveyed herself in the large oval mirror that hung upon the wall above her marble-topped dressing table while she arranged the small hat at a most becoming angle. It matched the color of her dress. One side was tilted off her face while a white plume drooped over the dark mass of her hair.

She smiled as she saw her reflection in the mirror. It was a satisfied smile, the self-satisfied smile of a vain young creature who exulted in her beauty and in the power which that beauty wielded over those she sought to charm.

Even an artist could have found no flaw in that beauty. Her eyes were large and black, lustrous and alluring when she chose to make them so and flaming with fire when her anger was aroused, as it often was, for her temper was quick and uncontrolled. Her small mouth, with the lips deep red, seemed made for kisses. The delicately arched brows and the dimpled chin gave no hint to any artist who might aspire to paint her, of the ruthlessness and the selfishness and heartlessness which lay beneath that lovely exterior.

Only those who knew her intimately—her family, the slaves who were often the victims of her wrath, and the men who had been attracted by her beauty—had found to their sorrow that there were tiger's claws beneath the harmless exterior that deceived the unwary.

The girl again smiled at her reflection, this time revealing the even white teeth. Then she laughed softly. How it had surprised Ralph when she had slapped him out there in the darkness at the party the other night. The simpleton! As if he couldn't see that she was encouraging him to do the very thing which had caused him to be slapped. She had been so coy when he had asked her to slip outside with him while the others were playing that silly game, and she had yielded to his request with every pretense of breathless excitement. She was being very unconventional, for it was not proper for a young lady of eighteen to slip out into dark gardens with a young man whom she had not known long. She should remain under the watchful eye of the chaperones at the party. But, she argued, what nonsense to be a slave to conventions. Who dictated conventions anyway? Probably some sour old maid who had never had the chance for romance.

What was the use of being beautiful, if a girl couldn't enjoy the power this beauty gave her, to know the thrill of being held in some handsome man's arms and to feel the touch of his eager lips upon hers? If she should have to wait until she was engaged for this to happen, how dull it would be in the meantime! And if the right man never came along, then perhaps she would be like that old maid who had decreed all those rules and regulations for the proper behavior of the very young. Her youth and beauty would have been wasted.

She and Ralph had gone out under the trees where the lights from the parlors shone dimly and Ralph had lost no time in declaring his love. It had been so easy to capture this boy's heart. He had just moved to the city recently and her beauty had made a slave of him from the beginning. She had listened to his ardent declaration while he held her hand. She allowed him to draw her closer while she looked into his eyes and saw in them his desire. She knew that he was going to kiss her and she did not stop him. He should have asked permission, according to the code of those silly conventions, but he had not thought about codes just then. He had taken her in his arms and held her close. She could feel the mad pounding of his heart and her own answered in the thrill of this moment. Then he had kissed her. She had rested her warm lips for a moment against his eager, clinging caress, then, with a quick dramatic gesture, she had torn herself from his arms and given him a resounding slap.

His mouth flew open in astonishment and his anger flared. "Why did you do that?" he demanded.

"As if you had to ask," she retorted scornfully. "You had no right to kiss me."

He laughed, his scorn matching hers. "No right! You gave

me the right. You gave me every encouragement to kiss you.
You led me on to kiss you. What kind of a girl are you,
anyway?"

"I'm not the kind who permits a man to kiss her without her permission," she replied loftily.

She was surprised at his reaction to that slap. She felt at a
distinct disadvantage. Instead of giving him the tongue lash-
ing she had intended to give him, she was on the defensive and
the experience was new.

"That is quite amusing, Mistress Wilborn," Ralph remarked sarcastically. "I didn't need to ask your permission.
You wanted me to kiss you and you know it. You are a heartless flirt and I despise you. You led me on because you knew
that I fell a victim to your beauty from the moment I met you.
Now that I know you for what you are, I thank you for revealing your true self to me and liberating me from a love that
would have given me nothing but heartache. I bid you good
evening, Mistress Wilborn."

He turned and left her standing there feeling furious and
defeated and humiliated. She slipped back into the house hoping that her absence had not been discovered.

The smile faded from her lips this morning as Diana recalled the end of that little escapade. She tossed her head as
she turned away from the mirror and went to the door of her
sister's room, to see whether she was still asleep. Ralph was but
an incident, though a very surprising one at that, she had to
confess. Most of her affairs had ended quite differently. No
matter. He would not forget her so easily. She would see to
that. He'd still be one of her company of victims. If he should
prove a still greater surprise by not remaining one, she would
forget him.

She stood in the doorway looking down at her younger sister who was still sleeping. Angela was quite pretty, Diana had
to admit, with her golden-brown hair, the deep blue eyes and
the same features that both had inherited from their mother.
Perhaps a little too babyish, Diana thought, as she considered
the sleeping girl, no match for her own dark, flaming beauty

and of course no rival for that beauty in the field of conquest. But then Angela did not possess the instincts of the huntress which marked herself. She was quiet and gentle, adored by all the servants and loved by her host of friends because of her sweetness and her thoughtfulness. She was gay and full of the joy of living, but there was no vanity within her. She seemed unconscious of her beauty, for Diana's sparkle and loveliness apparently overshadowed her own lesser charm. Angela loved her older sister and admired her beauty and there was no spark of jealousy when Diana seemed to be always surrounded by admirers who overlooked Angela entirely.

Diana smiled tenderly at the sleeping girl, then she tiptoed over the thick carpet and down the winding stairway that led to the large reception hall at the foot. The newel post with its gleaming brass mercury holding a lighted torch, bore the evidence of recent polishing, while the crystal chandeliers in the living room and the reception hall glistened in the sunlight which peeped through the lace curtains between the rich folds of the heavy drapes at the high windows.

In the dining room just back of the living room Diana could see Gertie, the dining room maid, setting the table for breakfast while the faint odor of bacon and coffee came through the open door.

The house had belonged to the Wilborn family for generations. Roger Wilborn, the present owner, had spared nothing in the furnishing of the home to make it beautiful and comfortable. The broad front porch was flanked by Ionian pillars that rose from the ground to the high roof of the upper balcony. The path leading to the front gate was too shady for flowers, but beyond where the sunlight could reach them, there were flowers growing in profusion. Shrubs dotted the lawn which spread far on either side of the house.

Diana closed the front door gently so as not to disturb anyone and descended the steps to the mounting block where a young slave boy stood waiting with her horse. The horse was a beautiful chestnut thoroughbred, a spirited animal, but well trained and responsive to her slightest touch or command.

She mounted the block with the help of the slave and sprang lightly into the saddle. The horse was eager to be off at a gallop but she held him to a slow pace until she reached the front gate as the slave ran ahead to open it.

"You'd better wait here until I return," she told him. "I shall not be gone long and they will be waiting breakfast for me."

"Yes'm," the boy replied as he closed the gate and sat down upon the grass nearby.

Diana was an expert horsewoman and she let the horse have the reins for a while as he galloped past the borders of her father's plantation. The young sugar cane was spreading waving carpets of slender green leaves over the broad acres of the plantation as far as the eye could see. This was one of the largest and most prosperous plantations in that part of the state and the beautiful home and the acres of growing cane, with the cabins of the slaves and the sugar mill in the rear, was one of the scenic spots along the river above the city.

When Diana left her father's property the road led through a wooded section for a short distance before approaching the borders of the next plantation. She checked the reins and the horse slowed to a gentle pace while the girl's eager eyes scanned the scene ahead of her, the neglected garden and the house which showed signs of much needed repairs. The door was open and her inquiring gaze sought for some sign of the occupant. There was no sign of anyone about, so she rode on slowly. She was disappointed, yet she admitted to herself that it might be too early for anyone to be up and about and that if she did catch a glimpse of the owner, it would be only a fleeting and unsatisfactory one. But curiosity had brought her out here on this early morning ride. She was anxious to see the new owner of the plantation.

She wondered what Keith Roland would be like. If he was handsome and interesting she would be glad to have him as a neighbor and a friend, even if he did come from the North and even if he might be a potential enemy. If he was neither handsome nor interesting, she could hate him as much as she did anything or anyone who was connected with that section of the country north of the Mason and Dixon line.

It was a critical time in the land, with bitterness and hatred rapidly reaching the boiling point, when states' rights and the cry for abolition were about to divide a nation which, under God, was destined to become the leading power of a world which was clamoring for freedom.

Diana was ardent in her love for the Southland and in her hatred of the North which seemed determined to strip them of their possessions in human lives. But she would be willing to forget that hatred for at least this one who had lived in the North, if he proved sufficiently interesting. The game of love and the conquest of hearts was something entirely removed from the game of war.

She rode on for a while before deciding to turn around and head for home. She was sitting relaxed in the saddle while she thought about the young man who had just come to take possession of his grandfather's estate when suddenly, from out of nowhere it seemed, a huge dog bounded down the road, barking savagely with frightening, deep-throated emphasis. The charge was so unexpected and so terrifying that both horse and rider were caught unawares. The horse reared and plunged so suddenly to one side to escape the beast that Diana, sitting relaxed and unprepared for the sudden movement, was thrown from the horse and tumbled in a most unbecoming heap in the middle of the dusty road.

She was stunned for a moment by the sudden fall and lay there inert. She did not see the horseman who halted his horse suddenly nearby and hastened to her. When she opened her eyes he was bending over her and looking at her with deep concern.

"I'm terribly sorry!" he exclaimed as he saw her eyes open and knew that she was conscious. "I do hope you're not seriously hurt. I wouldn't have had this happen for anything in the world. Do you think you can stand? I do hope you're not hurt badly."

Without waiting for her to speak he put his arm around her

and helped her to her feet. She stood rather wobbly for a moment, then jerked herself from his arms and faced him with blazing eyes. Her hat lay in the dust while her hair had fallen in a dark shining mass about her shoulders. She was covered with dust and even her face was streaked with it.

"I'm not hurt, no thanks to you and that dratted dog! He might have killed me."

The young man couldn't keep back the smile. Her voice was imperious but she looked ridiculous. Yet she was very beautiful, even at that, he commented mentally. Those blazing eyes, though so scornful, were lovely and her slender figure had grace in every line, even though that riding habit was a sorry mess.

"I realize that," he said contritely, as contritely as he could manage with the smile still lingering upon his lips. He could afford to smile since she did not seem to be hurt. "May I repeat that I'm terribly sorry. I didn't know that Bruce was out. I never dreamed that he could jump that fence."

"He should be chained, or better still, shot!" she cried wrathfully. "It's no fault of his that I don't have a broken neck. Just look at me! This dress is ruined and I'm a fright."

"You're a very beautiful fright, Mistress Wilborn," he replied gallantly. "This is certainly not a very propitious time for introductions, but I'm Keith Roland, your new neighbor. I do hope that you can forgive this unfortunate beginning and that we can be friends. I'd like very much to be friends."

She eyed him speculatively. He was quite handsome, in fact as handsome as any man she had ever known. His gray eyes under their level brows waited for her answer while his mouth with the firm chin still held the faint smile which had lingered there. His brown hair had been ruffled by the breeze and fell over his forehead in an unruly mass which he brushed carelessly back while he waited for her to speak. He was quite tall and slender, but there was no hint of thinness about his well proportioned figure.

"I'll consider it, if you'll keep that dog chained so that he can't run around frightening people," she finally conceded.

"I shall see that he is properly housed so that this can never happen again," he assured her. "I can't understand why he should have barked at you. He never does that. He's really a friendly dog, even though he is huge and vicious looking. Perhaps the spring fever got in his blood. He's new here and he must have been out investigating the surroundings. I thought he was safe at home."

"Well, I warn you that if he ever sets foot on my place, I'll have him shot. I hate dogs and this one in particular."

His face became grave as the smile vanished.

"That would certainly be unfortunate," he told her. "Bruce is as dear to me as if he were human and if anyone killed him, I would feel that he would have murdered one of my family, in fact the only one left of my family. So don't try it, Mistress Wilborn."

She felt rebuked and her eyes blazed again. She was not used to being rebuked. Usually it was she who did the rebuking when she felt it necessary. She saw that the smile that had made him so attractive had faded. His mouth could look grim and it did so now, much to her discomfort.

"Would you be kind enough to get my horse?" she asked, pretending to ignore his remark.

He got the horse which was grazing quietly not far away and brought it to her.

"If you will allow me, I will take you to my house and have one of the maids help you get cleaned up," he offered as he held her bridle.

"Thank you, no," she retorted in her most haughty manner. "Help me on my horse, if you will."

He held out his hands, cupped for her small foot. She put her foot in them and he gave her a boost into the saddle, then handed her the crumpled and dust-covered hat. She took it and without a word, turned and galloped away, her hair streaming in the wind as she rode.

Keith stood looking after her while the dog came up and nuzzled his hand. The dog had stood watching the scene, scarcely moving a muscle, as if he sensed the tenseness in the atmosphere and stood ready to defend his master if the occasion required it. Keith patted the animal's head gently and Bruce whined softly while his tail wagged slowly.

"A spoiled little brat, if there ever was one," he remarked. "If she's a sample of what the rest of the family is like, I don't think I'm going to enjoy my neighbors." He turned to the dog. "Bruce, old fellow, you've gotten me into a pretty mess. What on earth made you do such a silly thing?"

Bruce gave a faint woof as he cast adoring eyes upon his master.

Keith shrugged and turned to his horse and mounted slowly. No matter what the outcome of this unpleasant incident, there was nothing he could do more than he had done. What couldn't be helped must be endured. But he was disappointed. He had looked forward to meeting the Wilborns. He had heard much of Diana and her family from his friends in New Orleans, the Mayhew family, and he had hoped that they could enjoy many pleasant hours together during the coming summer. Now he was not sure that he would be welcome in their home. He dismounted at the steps of his house and turned his horse over to a young Negro boy who came bounding to meet him when he rode through the gate.

2

THE YOUNG SLAVE BOY ran to open the gate when he saw Diana galloping down the road. He stared at her with wide eyes and open mouth as she rode past him at top speed. He ran as fast as he could but she was waiting impatiently for him when he reached the mounting block. She gave him the reins and mounted the steps, then opened the door, went inside and shut it with a bang. She hoped that the family would be in the dining room and would not see what a fright she was.

The breakfast bell had just sounded and the three of them,

Roger Wilborn and his wife, Alicia, and Angela were on their way down the stairs. When they saw Diana so disheveled and so angry, they stopped and stared at her in speechless surprise. Angela was the first to break the amazed silence.

"Sis! What a fright you are!" She broke out laughing. "Don't tell me you let Prancer throw you!"

"Angela!" her mother rebuked her. "You shouldn't laugh at her. She may be hurt. Are you hurt, dear?" she asked solicitously.

She went to Diana and attempted to put an arm around her, but the girl drew away.

"Don't touch me, Mother. You'll get your dress dirty. I'll change and be down in a minute. Don't wait breakfast for me."

"What happened?" her father asked.

"That Yankee's dratted dog frightened Prancer and he threw me," she cried wrathfully. "He should know better than to let a brute like that run loose on the road. I could have had my neck broken, no thanks to him."

Her father came closer and spoke sternly.

"I've warned you before, Diana, about using such language. No matter what the provocation, there is no excuse for that. It's not becoming to any girl. It cheapens her and I don't want you to appear cheap, even in the eyes of the servants. You've got to learn to control your temper."

"Oh Father!" she cried impatiently. "Is this a time for lectures? I'm not hurt seriously, but I'm bruised and shaken and I have a right to be angry. Wouldn't you be if you had made a spectacle of yourself in front of that Yankee? No doubt he thinks we are all cheap and ignorant, so what if I did lose my temper before him? Please let me go and get cleaned up."

They stood aside to let her pass while her mother said, "We'll wait for you, dear, so don't be too long."

While Diana mounted the steps she heard Angela's giggle as the three went into the dining room. The little brat! She'd love to give her a good shaking. As sweet as Angela was, she did love to tease and teasing was something that Diana could not take gracefully. There were tears in her eyes as she went to her room and began to change her clothes. The tears running down amid the dust did not add to her attractiveness and what she saw in the mirror caused them to flow faster.

What a miserable failure this morning's outing had proved! She had dressed so carefully so that she might charm this new neighbor if she should happen to meet him. Well, she had met him and what a fright she was when he saw her. She felt ashamed of her outburst of temper and she wished with all her heart that she could wipe out that moment. He would think the worst of her and when he had seen her there was no beauty that he could admire — such a dust-covered, disheveled termagant!

There was no time for tears, for the family was waiting for her, so she washed her face hurriedly and brushed her hair rapidly, then tied a ribbon about it, letting it hang loosely about her shoulders. She slipped on a clean gingham dress and joined the three in the dining room. Her mother greeted her with a smile as she took her place at the table.

"You look as fresh and lovely as if you'd just come from a dew-drenched garden," she remarked.

"Mother! You're getting poetic," Angela remarked. "I'm glad you were not hurt, Sis, and I'm sorry if I laughed, but you did look comical. I never saw you look like that before and I just couldn't help it. I look like that so often, all dirty and tousled, when I've been out playing with the animals, but you never do."

Diana refused to answer but gave Angela a withering look. She was still thinking of that scene on the roadside and wondering what Keith Roland would think of her.

"We have cream cheese this morning," her mother remarked, as the maid brought in the hot coffee and the biscuits upon a silver tray covered with a white linen cloth. "That ought to bring a smile."

Diana managed a smile and a fond look at her mother. "It does," she said.

They bowed their heads while Roger gave thanks for what they were about to receive. He added a thanksgiving that

Diana had not been hurt and had returned safely. Diana felt the sting of tears as she heard her father's prayer, for though she was rebellious and willful and quick tempered, she loved her parents devotedly and she knew how much her father loved her. He could not conceal the fact that Diana was his idol. He loved both of his children, of course, but Diana had been born when they had almost despaired of ever having any children and he felt that she had come to them in answer to prayer. She was so beautiful even as a tiny baby, and, as a small child, she had known how to use that beauty to capture hearts. She had his heart twined about her baby fingers and he spoiled her even over the protest of his wife who saw the danger in such indulgence.

As she grew older Roger realized his mistake, for Diana seemed absolutely without any desire to give her heart and soul to the Lord. It grieved him and he and his wife prayed constantly that one day she would yield her life to the Lord whom they loved and served. As she grew older, she seemed to grow farther and farther away instead of yielding. Her one desire was to exploit her beauty and use it to enslave the hearts of men. She lived only for pleasure.

When Angela was a small child she had accepted Christ as her Saviour and though she was full of fun and was somewhat of a tomboy when it came to climbing trees and romping with the young farm animals, she loved the Lord and her one desire was to live for Him. Though she loved her sister, she saw how vain and selfish Diana was and an impish little desire rose within her quite often to tease Diana and ruffle her vanity. This morning had been one of those times.

"Just what happened to make your horse throw you?" Roger asked while they ate.

"I had just passed the Roland place when a big brute of of a dog came bounding down the road from behind a clump of bushes and headed straight for Prancer. His bark sounded like the roar of a lion. It took us both by surprise. I had let the reins loose for he was going slowly and I was sitting relaxed. He was so frightened that he jumped and reared up and I tumbled in the dust."

"Then I suppose Mr. Roland came to the rescue like Sir Lancelot and saved you from the monster," Angela suggested with a giggle.

"How did you guess?" Diana asked loftily, while her eyes flashed fire in contrast to her cold tone.

"Angela!" her mother cried. "This is no time for teasing."

"I'm sorry, Mother," Angela replied meekly, "but surely someone must have come along to help you back on your horse. Was it Mr. Roland?"

"Yes, it was," Diana retorted crossly. "He apologized for what that brute had done. He said he didn't know the dog could jump the high fence. I told him that animal should be shot."

"I suppose you displayed your temper as usual," her father remarked while his reproving gaze rested upon her.

"I suppose I did," she admitted.

"I wonder what he'll think of us," Roger said with a sigh and a shake of his head. "He'll no doubt think that I've been a very poor parent to have a daughter who could forget that she was a lady when he did all he could to atone for what happened."

"I wonder what he'll think of me," Diana was saying to herself. Aloud she said humbly, "I'm so sorry, Father. I just forgot myself. But I was so shaken up that I scarcely knew what I was saying. I looked such a fright and I was bruised, even though he never knew it. My side is black and blue."

There were tears in her eyes but Angela knew that those tears were for her father, that she might temper his disapproval with sympathy.

"He probably thinks that we're all ignorant and unmannerly, I suppose," Diana remarked as her father's grave eyes continued to regard her. "But then," she continud with a toss of her head, "isn't that what all Yankees think of us in the South?"

"Diana, Mr. Roland isn't really a Yankee," Angela informed her. "He was born here in the South and he lived right there on that plantation when he was a little fellow. He went to live in the North when his father and his grandfather had a quarrel. So perhaps some of the South is still in his blood, even if he did just come from the North."

"How did you become so well informed about him?" Diana asked in surprise.

Angela gave her a mischievous smile.

"By asking a lot of questions. He was staying with the Mayhews, you know, when he first arrived. Mr. Mayhew and Keith's father were old friends. Dot Mayhew told me all about him. She thinks he's very handsome and such a polished gentleman. She couldn't talk of anything else but him and of course I was willing to listen."

The maid cleared the breakfast dishes and brought in cream cheese in a blue glass bowl. It was one of the favorite dishes of the family. The soft curd which had been molded in round tin molds until most of the whey had dripped out, was covered with rich sour cream. They ate it lavishly sprinkled with sugar. It was Diana's favorite dish.

"Father," Angela said presently, "don't you think it would be a very friendly gesture if you would invite Mr. Roland over for dinner some evening? Especially since he might have a very bad opinion of us?"

Her father smiled indulgently at her.

"Especially since he is such a very handsome and polished gentleman? You wouldn't want to be trying to take him away from Dot, would you?"

"I wouldn't know until I had seen him," Angela countered with a roguish smile. "But we could at least show him that we can be polite and polished also — and charming when there are no dogs around to frighten us."

Roger laughed softly. "You're irrepressible," he remarked. Then he became serious. "I hope, little one, that nothing will ever come up to kill that effervescent spirit, but don't let it lead you too far. I think your sister has had all the teasing she can take for this morning."

"I wouldn't hurt you for the world, Sis," Angela said as

she rose and went around the table and gave Diana a hug. "I love you and I think you're the most beautiful girl in all the world. That ought to take the fire out of those eyes and bring a smile to your lips."

She kissed Diana upon her cheek. Diana smiled at her as Angela returned to her chair. She was somewhat mollified by Angela's extravagant compliment.

"I do love to ruffle your feathers, though," Angela said with a sly little smile. "It's such fun to see your eyes flash and your lip curl. You're very pretty even then. How I wish I could have seen you out there when Mr. Roland picked you up. What a shock both of you must have had!"

"Let's be serious," her mother admonished. "It's time for your father to read from the Bible."

Roger opened his Bible at the passage in Matthew from the Sermon on the Mount, ending with the verse, "Love your enemies, bless them that curse you, do good to them that hate you, pray for them that despitefully use you and persecute you."

When he had finished and had offered a short prayer for their guidance through the day, Diana looked at him with questioning eyes.

"Do you really believe that we should do what that verse says we should?" she asked.

"Of course," her father replied. "Those are the words of Jesus."

"Do you think it is possible to do that? I don't."

"God would never tell us to do anything that was impossible," he told her gravely. "Perhaps it may not be easy, but it is possible, though only through the strength and the grace that God gives to those whose hearts belong to Him. To the unbeliever it may not be possible, but to those who love the Lord, it is possible and God demands it of us."

"Then that means that we must love those drat — forgive me, those pesky Yankees who are trying to take our rights away from us. How can we do that? They are doing everything they can to goad us into war, yet you say that we must love them."

He smiled, rather ruefully, it is true.

"You have put a very difficult question to me, my child. It is hard for us to see eye to eye with those of the North who fail to see that if we are forced to let all the slaves go free at once, it would destroy our economy and wreck us, but that does not mean that we should have hatred in our hearts for them."

"But if war should come, what would you feel about that? Would you feel that it was right to go out and kill them?"

"War is never right, my child. It has never settled any issue yet, only created bitterness and suffering. But if war should come and the demand was made upon us to fight for our land and what we think is right, every man who had any sense of loyalty would be forced to feel that he should obey the call of his country. Killing is a terrible thing, even in war, but a soldier can kill to defend his land against an invader even without hate in his heart for an individual. He could kill an enemy even while he felt pity for that individual and even though his whole soul might revolt against taking a human life. I hope that we will never be called upon to fight against those of our own nation. War against different nations is bad enough, but war within a nation is a terrible thing. I pray that it will never be inflicted upon us."

"Let's forget about war," Angela suggested. "I don't believe it will come to us. You haven't said whether you would invite Mr. Roland over to dinner, Father. Couldn't we try to make a friend of him instead of wondering whether he would become our enemy right here in our midst?"

"I think your idea is a good one," he told her. "We'll invite him over one evening real soon. Would that make you happy?"

"Very! And it would please Diana too, I'm sure. It would give her a chance to show him how beautiful she really is when she's nice and clean and how charming she can be when she's not angry."

They rose from the table and Angela fled from the room as Diana pretended to chase her with upraised arm.

3

W HEN THE FAMILY SEPARATED after breakfast, Diana went
to her room to wash her hair, for it was still full of dust. She
was glad that Angela had suggested inviting Keith to dinner.
Now that her anger had cooled, she was thoroughly ashamed
of her exhibition of temper and she dreaded to imagine what
Keith would think of her. She wanted the chance to make
amends and to try to win his friendship. Since she had seen
him and knew that Dot Mayhew's description of him was not
exaggerated, she was more than casually interested, even though
she had thought him one of those "pesky" Yankees. The fact
that he was born in the South effaced some of the scorn with
which she had regarded him even when her curiosity had led
her out upon the road to such a humiliating encounter. He was
older than the other young men of her acquaintance and it
would be exciting to see whether her charms could add him
to her company of admirers. She hoped that her father would
invite him soon.

Roger left the house to look after the work in the field. He
had a good overseer, a slave who had been born on the place
and had worked for his father until his death. Roger loved the
place where he had been born and where he grew up and he
loved to ride over the acres of cane and watch it as it grew to
maturity and was ready for the cutting and grinding.

Some distance from the hou.. there was a vegetable garden and an enclosure where chickens and pigs were kept. Beyond that a few cows had an enclosed grazing ground. It took
quite a lot of vegetables and meat to feed the slaves and Roger
saw that his people were well provided for.

Back at the plantation house, Alicia went into the
kitchen to make out the menu for the luncheon and dinner.
Mammy Sue, the old Negro who had nursed Roger and both
of his girls, was too old to do much work, but she sat like a

queen in the kitchen when the meals were being prepared and lorded it over the other servants. They accepted her and her orders without complaint for they knew that she was a privileged character in the family. They also knew that even though she felt it her right to instruct them with their cooking and the way they managed the kitchen, that she lived what she professed to be, a humble follower of the Lord whom she had served since she was a small child. If any one of them were sick or needed help of some kind, Mammy Sue was the one who was always there first to give what help she could. When a new baby came, it was she who was on hand to help with the child and with the mother. And whenever there was sorrow or death, she was there to sit by the sufferer's bed or to comfort a grieving heart with her sympathy and her knowledge of the Word.

She could read fairly well and she would often sit beside someone who was ill and read to them from her Bible, stumbling over the more difficult words. She had led many of them to the Lord.

Angela loved her devotedly. Mammy Sue had been her nurse and the child had first learned of the love of God from her. When she had been cross and fretful, Mammy Sue had soothed and entertained her by telling her stories from the Bible and Angela had grown up with a child's knowledge of the Book which she later learned to love because she had become acquainted with its Author.

Diana had been willful and impatient of the old woman's attempts to lead her to know the Lord and as soon as she had become old enough not to need her as a nurse, she had refused to remain in the old slave's care. By that time Angela had been born and Mammy Sue had given all of her attention to the new baby.

Angela went to the kitchen as soon as she had escaped from Diana's pursuit which had ended at the foot of the stairs. She waited until her mother had finished with the cook and the maid, then she went over and stood beside Mammy Sue.

"You don't have to stay in the kitchen any longer now,"

she said. "It's such a nice warm day we can go out on the back porch and have a long talk before I go down and see how the young colt is and help Tom feed the chickens. I think Nora and Gertie can get along without you for a little while." She gave the two Negro women a wink and a smile which they returned surreptitiously.

"All right, chile, let's get out of here." Mammy Sue rose slowly and followed Angela out to the wide back porch.

The porch was latticed in where the morning sun shone upon it, but the other part was open to the lovely flower garden which was a blaze of color in the early spring. Larkspur and geraniums mingled in a pattern of red and blue, while early lilies opened their white petals on the tall slender stalks that bordered the bed. Mocking birds trilled in the trees nearby while sparrows twittered and quarreled as they searched for worms among the flowers and on the grass. The occasional rasping squawk of a blue jay marred the lovely songs of the mocking birds and the warble of the little wrens as they busied themselves building their nests.

"What shall we read this morning?" Angela asked as they sat together on the swing.

"I feels lak praisin' de Lawd today," Mammy Sue replied. "This here's such a beautiful day. Everythin' is so peaceful and every one is gettin' along so good. Ain't nobody sick and dey all seems to be happy and satisfied. It jest look lak de Lawd is smilin' down on all of us folks."

"I wish it could stay this way," Angela sighed. "If everyone loved the Lord like you do, Mammy, then perhaps every day would be like this one and everyone would always be happy and contented."

"But de debbil sees to dat, honey. He ain't aimin' to let dis ole world have peace and happiness 'till de Lawd comes back and puts him in dat pit where he belong. I hope I lives to see dat day, honey, but dis ole body is gittin' mighty feeble and I'se afeared dat de Lawd gwine to call me home befo' dat day comes."

"I hope He doesn't call you home for a long time, Mammy,"

Angela said and patted the old Negro's hand. "I need you here with me. Even Mother can't talk to me like you do. Somehow I can talk to you about the Lord and tell you things that are on my heart which I can't tell her, even though she is a Christian and I love her so much."

"Dat's because I done raised you, chile, and 'cause I done led you to de Lawd. Yo' Ma is got lots on her mind and she got work to do while I'se got nothin' but you and them trifling gals in de kitchen."

Angela smiled at her mention of the trifling girls in the kitchen, for they were well trained and the cook was an expert.

Together they read the last three Psalms which were a continuous paean of praise. Mammy Sue stumbled over some of the words but Angela corrected her as they read together. Then they prayed and Angela left for the farmyard to help feed the chickens and to romp with the young colt.

She was still a childish tomboy in some respects, in spite of her sixteen years. She was trying to train a small colt, young as it was, to do a few simple tricks. The little animal loved her and came obediently to her call, though the mother looked with anxious eyes as Angela put the colt through his paces. Angela owned a small dog which was not allowed in the house very often while they were on the plantation, for the little animal romped over the place and dug holes in the earth and was often too dirty to be taken inside, in spite of the frequent washings which Angela gave him. In the winter when the family moved to the city, he was a dignified and proper house pet, much to Diana's disgust, for she did not like pets of any kind.

Angela was having so much fun helping to gather the eggs and to feed the stock, that lunch time slipped up on her and she had to race to the house when the bell sounded. She came in out of breath and with her hair flying in a golden-brown cloud about her face, with cheeks red from running and eyes bright and lips parted in a smile of the joy and exuberance of youth.

Diana regarded her with a disapproving glance.

"What a way to come to the table!" she exclaimed. "You look more like a farm hand than one of the family."

Angela smiled as she bent her head and gave her sister a sidelong glance.

"That's just what I am, a farm hand and I love it! I've fed the chickens, slopped the pigs, gathered the eggs and washed Toby. Then I gave Little Fellow a few lessons in tricks and now I have a good appetite, as all farm hands should have. What's wrong with that?"

Her mother came in just then and overheard her reply. She gave her youngest daughter an indulgent smile as she said, "Even farm hands clean up before they eat. How about washing your face and combing your hair? Your father will like it better if you do."

"She knows that," Diana remarked disdainfully as Angela flew up the stairs, taking two at a bound.

She returned a few moments later with her hair held in place by a ribbon and held out her hands for her mother's inspection.

"Will the boss be pleased with these?" She grinned at her mother and leaned over and kissed her impulsively. "This is such a glorious day that I could almost burst for joy at just being alive. Isn't God good to give us so much to be thankful for?"

"Yes, darling, He is," Alicia replied as they took their places about the table.

Roger came in with the paper which he had been reading. It had just been brought from town.

"Things aren't getting any better in the political situation," he remarked as he laid the paper down. "If Lincoln is elected, I'm afraid to think of what will happen to us. There will be war. He is too strong for abolition and the South will not stand for that."

"Oh Father, please, let's not spoil this beautiful day by talk of war," Angela exclaimed. "It will spoil my appetite and I'm hungry as a bear."

"I promise not to." He gave her a smile as he bowed his

head and then returned thanks. "Talking won't change conditions," he continued as they began to eat, "and worrying won't help matters, so we'll forget politics and enjoy the good things the Lord has provided for us."

The luncheon was lavish, as it always was. There were waffles and broiled steak, fluffy whipped potatoes and sliced tomatoes. For dessert there was ginger bread cut in thick squares with a sauce of boiled sugar rich with butter.

"When are you planning to invite Mr. Roland over, Father?" Angela asked while they were eating their dessert. She had kept the conversation going by gay chatter with her father all during the meal. Her chatter was always interesting and her father enjoyed her effervescence which was never silly, but always full of humor.

"You never give up, once you get an idea in that pretty little head of yours, do you?" he replied with an amused smile. "One would think that it was you who had fallen head over heels in love with that young man instead of Dot."

"How could I when I've never set eyes on him? I'm curious to see this paragon of good looks and charming manners. I think it would be wonderful to have him for a friend when he's so near at hand. That is, if Diana will consent to share him with me."

"How can I share what I don't have and don't want to possess?" Diana asked coldly.

Diana had been unusually quiet during the meal and her parents thought they knew the reason. She was, as usual, after one of her outbursts of temper, repentant and humiliated, but too proud and stubborn to own that she was, or to try to make amends for whatever she had done or said when she lost control of her temper.

"No, he doesn't belong to you yet, but I'm afraid that he will be like all the others. He'll belong to you and I won't have a chance to get even a peep from him. If I ever have an adorer of my own, I'll either have to wait until you get married and out of my way or go to some distant place where they never heard of Diana Wilborn."

"Oh be quiet! You make me tired!" Diana retorted as she laid down her napkin and gave her sister a flashing look from her dark eyes.

As they rose from the table, Angela put an arm around Diana and said laughingly, "Don't be angry, Sis. You're so beautiful that when there are any men around, I don't even get a glimpse from them. But I don't mind. I'm proud of you. When you've finally made your pick for a husband there'll be plenty of time for me to look over the ones who are left behind weeping. I'll try to comfort at least one of them."

Diana was pleased by Angela's flattery, though she had heard it so often before, for she knew it was sincere. She gave Angela a playful slap as they left the room.

Roger called after Angela. "I thought I'd invite Mr. Roland over tomorrow evening. Would that please your highness?"

"Sure would," Angela replied as she waved to him and went out once more to the work she loved.

4

DIANA WAS NERVOUS AND EXCITED over the prospective visit of Keith Roland, though she revealed no hint to the family of how she felt. When it was time to dress for dinner, she chose one of her new dresses, a lovely thing of dull blue, with small ruffles cascading down the back of the full skirt and with a cream lace collar at her throat. It suited her dark beauty and revealed the whiteness of her rounded arms and slim white throat.

She combed her hair high upon her head in a cluster of curls which cascaded down to the nape of her neck. This made her look older, but it was very becoming and at eighteen, she could afford to look older than her years. She knew that Keith was quite a few years older than she was and she felt that this might give her some advantage. She did not want him to look upon her as a child, for she had plans which no child would ever consider.

Angela came downstairs just behind Diana and her simple white dress with the tiny ruffles around the bottom of her skirt and bordering the round neck of her dress, made her look quite young and girlish. A wide black velvet ribbon was fastened about her waist with a big bow at one side. Her hair was caught loosely at the back with a black bow and curls hung about her shoulders, matching the eager brown eyes. She was very much excited over the impending visit and she did not try to conceal her excitement.

"Do you think he'll like me like this, Mother?" she asked as she pirouetted upon the tiptoes of her black slippers. "I do hope he will, for I know that I shall like him from what Dot told me."

"Don't be such a silly child, Angela," Diana said as she turned from the window where she stood. "What difference does it make what he thinks of us? It's what we will think of him that counts. He's still a Yankee, no matter how charming he might be."

"If it doesn't matter what he thinks of us, why did you go to such trouble to dress up for him?" Angela asked. "I never saw you take longer to primp, not even for one of your parties."

Diana flushed at the jibe.

"I want him to forget that I looked such a fright the first time he saw me," she explained rather lamely. "He will at least see that we Southerners know how to dress and that we are not all as ignorant as he may think we are."

Angela went to the window and stood beside Diana. There was a smile upon her face, a little knowing smile that betrayed the fact that she was not misled by Diana's flimsy excuse.

"I think he got a little idea of what some Southerners are like, from the Mayhews," she remarked. "I'm sure that they gave him a very good impression."

"Here he comes now, so get away from the window," Diana

said. "Don't let him see us staring at him." She left the window and sat down nearby.

"He must have good eyes if he can see us this far," Angela retorted. "He's riding a beautiful bay and he rides like an expert. That's one thing in his favor. I hope he'll ask me to go riding with him one of these days. That would be wonderful."

She caught the glint in Diana's eyes as she left the window and sat down upon the tufted sofa near the door, but she said nothing. She knew her sister so well that she believed she could read Diana's mind. She sighed as they waited for the visitor to arrive. What was the use of hoping to have this neighbor for a friend? Diana already had designs upon him and she herself would never have a chance to enjoy a ride or anything with him.

After what seemed ages they heard the front doorbell ring and Nora went to open the door. Roger met Keith in the hall and extended a welcome to him.

"We're so glad to have you as our guest," he said. "I'm Roger Wilborn and this is my wife," he added as Alicia came out to meet him.

"It was so kind of you to invite me," Keith told him. "I confess that life is rather lonely for me over there in that big house all alone. I was hoping that we might become acquainted, but I didn't want to barge in on you without being invited."

"You can thank Angela for thinking of having you over," Roger told him as they entered the parlor. "This is my daughter Angela. Allow me to introduce Mr. Roland, Angela."

Angela was already coming forward to meet them. He bowed before her as she gave him her hand and he gave her a smile.

"Thank you for being so thoughtful about inviting me so soon," he said.

"Father would have done it without my suggestion. He's just trying to tease me," she told him with a smile.

Diana stood cool and aloof though she was angry and impatient because she had been ignored while Angela had been introduced.

Roger turned to her and remarked, "I believe you have met my oldest daughter, Diana."

She gave him a radiant smile as she said, "Under very embarrassing circumstances, which I hope you will forget." She extended her hand and he bowed over it, then followed them to a seat which Alicia indicated.

"I'll have your horse taken care of," Roger remarked and left to give instructions to the stable boy.

"This place is so beautiful that it makes my place look more run down and shabby than ever," Keith remarked as a brief silence fell between them.

"I suppose it was hard for an old man to keep the place up all alone," Alicia replied. "He was alone so long and so feeble that he couldn't do much to keep it in repair."

"I think he lost the desire after my grandmother died. They were so devoted and had lived together for so long."

"I tried to help him with his planting," Roger remarked as he came into the room, "but he insisted that he was fully able to do his own overseeing, so I had to let him alone. He seemed to withdraw into himself and he was dead and buried before we knew that he was gone. I was sorry, for he and my father had been friends for many years."

"I think he grieved for my father more than he would admit," Keith said.

"Your father left for the North and never returned. We all thought it strange when he had everything that he could wish for here."

"He left because my grandfather ordered him to leave," Keith told him with a touch of sadness in his voice.

"Oh, I didn't know," Roger said apologetically. "I didn't mean to pry into family affairs, but I felt so sorry for the old man there all alone and so helpless."

"He was alone by his own stubborn desire. You may as well hear the whole story, for I don't want you to think unjustly of my father. He was as fine a man as ever lived. He and my mother were Christians. My grandmother was also a Christian, but my grandfather was a stubborn unbeliever until the day of his death, as far as I know. He and my father had a quarrel because my grandfather was planning to sell a slave, a young Negro who had a family there on the plantation. My father told him that it would be cruel to separate husband and wife when there was no need for doing such a cruel thing. My grandfather was furious at my father's accusation. He was offered a high price for the slave, for he was a skilled hand, and my grandfather insisted that he needed the money. The more they argued, the more furious my grandfather became. He ordered my father to leave the place and never return. My father said he was sorry if he had made him angry, but that what he had said was the truth and he couldn't change the way he felt. He begged my grandfather to reconsider, but he would not, so there was nothing for my father to do but leave and we never saw him again. My father wrote letter after letter, asking his forgiveness but he would not even answer those letters. My father came back once to try to talk to him, but the old man would not even let him in the house. I think grief finally hastened my father's death. When the old man died, we learned that he had left the place to me. I suppose he did that to spite my father, but he really left me with a white elephant on my hands. I don't know a thing about farm life and I'm afraid I'll never make a go of it."

"I'll be glad to help you in any way that I can," Roger offered.

"Thank you. I'm sure that I'll need your advice about many things."

"You were an army man, a graduate of West Point, were you not?" Angela asked.

"Yes. I was graduated from there and served my time in the army. I was just out last year. But how did you know?"

She gave him a smile while her brown eyes were full of mischief. "I've been doing a little bit of detective work," she told him.

He responded to her humor at once.

"Am I to be given the third degree?"

She laughed. "No. I have a full account of your life

from Dot Mayhew. At least as much as you gave to her. She and I are chums. Naturally I wanted to find out what our new neighbor was like, so — I asked her.",

"I hope that she gave you a good report about me."

"Oh, she did. The best. That's why I was anxious for us to become acquainted so that I could tell you how glad we are to have you for our neighbor."

"I'm sure that Mr. Roland can't be interested in your gossip with Dot," Diana remarked.

"But I am," Keith insisted. "I think that is about the nicest thing I've heard since I came here. It's been a long time since anyone has ever told me that they wanted to have me for a friend."

Angela felt humiliated by Diana's rebuke and it hurt her. The smile faded from her lips and the gleam from her eyes.

"I'm sorry if I have said anything I shouldn't have, Mr. Roland," she said contritely, "but I didn't think that Dot and I were gossiping about you. I thought that gossip was when someone repeated some scandal or something not very nice about a person. What Dot told me was all good about you."

"You're right about that definition of gossip," he told her. "I'm glad that Dot had only nice things to say about me. I think she's a charming and lovely young lady."

"Thank you," Angela murmured. Then she smiled again. "How Dot will be thrilled when I tell her what you said about her!"

Just then the maid came to announce dinner and they rose as Roger led the way to the dining room.

The room was lighted with small lamps burning in the crystal chandelier hanging over the table, while on the table, covered with a lace tablecloth, were silver candlesticks that gave off a mellow light which was reflected in the crystal goblets and the gleaming silver.

Keith was seated opposite the two girls and he had ample time to give them a closer inspection while they conversed as the maid brought in the first course of the dinner. They were both lovely, he observed, though opposites in coloring as well as in disposition. Diana's dark, brilliant beauty would attract anyone at first glance, but there was a coldness about that beauty, even when the lustrous eyes gave a hint of allure. Angela, though not quite so beautiful, had a personality that was sparkling and so spontaneous that it attracted without her being aware of the charm she possessed. She would never lack for friends, he surmised with quick appraisal, even though her sister might attract the hearts and admiration of men in a way that Angela never would. She would not, because, perhaps, she would have no desire to attract them in that way. He sensed the warmth in Angela that Diana lacked.

He wondered if these conjectures were true. It would be interesting to find out how true they were. It would indeed be quite interesting, for he had to admit that the dark beauty of the girl who had been so rude such a short time before, attracted his admiration and commanded his interest, even though he suspected that she might be vain and shallow, as well as rude when her temper was aroused.

These thoughts and speculations came subconsciously as he joined in the conversation with the girls and their parents.

The first course was gumbo, the thick soup that all the natives enjoyed, whether or not they were Creole. The Wilborns were not of French ancestry, but they did like the rich Creole food. The soup was made with okra, tomatoes, onion and just enough red pepper to give it zest. It was cooked with small bits of ham, while shrimp and crabs added to the rich flavor of the soup. It was served with a generous pile of fluffy rice in the middle of each plate.

"This is the first time I've tasted gumbo since I was a little fellow," Keith remarked, "and it is even more delicious than I remember it. My grandfather's old cook used to fix it for him but where we lived it was impossible to get fresh sea food. This takes me back to happy days almost forgotten."

"I'm so glad you like it," Alicia told him. "I was afraid that our Southern cooking might be too highly seasoned for you."

"I still have a lot of the South in my blood and I still love it," he replied.

There was a shade of seriousness in his voice which Angela was quick to notice. She wondered if he was thinking of the quarrel which had separated his family and brought such sorrow to his father.

The dinner was delicious and Keith seemed to enjoy every mouthful. The chicken was fried as only Nora could fry it — under Mammy's supervision, of course! There were candied yams and green peas and a tossed vegetable salad with a dressing that was like nothing Keith had ever tasted before. One of Mammy Sue's secrets, Angela informed him. For dessert there was charlotte russe served in little silver cups with lady fingers lining the inside and the rich confection rising in a white fluff above them.

"My cook seems to have lost the art of preparing inviting meals," Keith remarked as they ate. "Or perhaps she has lost the desire. It seems that just before I came here, the administrator of my estate sold one of her sons and she does not know where he is. I was angry when I found out about this, but the damage had been done and this fellow informed me that it had to be done to settle some pressing bills. I would gladly buy the boy back if I could find him, but there is no trace of him so far."

"That's the terrible thing about slavery," Roger remarked. "It's a crime in the sight of God for human beings to be sold like cattle with no regard for heartaches when families are separated. The Lord never intended for that to be."

Keith looked at his host in some surprise.

"I'm glad to hear you say that, sir, but I did not expect you to feel that way since you have been a slave owner and since you live here in the South where the subject is the cause of such bitter feeling and debate."

"I'm a Christian first and a Southerner next," Roger told him. "I have never felt that it was right to own slaves, even though I was raised here on this place where slaves have always been in my family. I feel that they should have their freedom and I have offered to set all of mine free. In fact I have written out their papers of freedom, but they have refused to leave. My father was always considerate of them and, as far as I know, never sold one. Families have grown up here from two generations back, so we have never bought any during my lifetime. Any time one of them wants to leave, he is free to do so, but they realize that they could never have what they have now if they were out in the world working for the wages they could earn. Here they have their families and their homes, all they need in the way of clothing and food and the work is never too hard, for I try to be considerate of them. They have returned my thoughtfulness by remaining here on the same basis as if they were in bondage, but knowing that they are free. That is, I'm sure, a wonderful thing for them to know."

Keith was silent a moment after this long speech, then he looked at Roger with a warm glow in his eyes.

"You make me proud to know you, sir, and I am honored to be counted as your friend."

"Thank you," Roger replied.

"You've given me an idea of how to get out of a very embarrassing situation with my own slaves. When I have known them well enough to have their confidence, I shall do the same thing with them, hoping that they will be as loyal to me as yours are to you, for I realize that without them I could not carry on with the plantation. I should have to sell out and I do not want to do that, for I love it here and hope to spend the rest of my life here."

"That is what I would have to do, if I had to pay the wages that they might demand," Roger replied. "It would ruin me. That is what the other planters in the South face if Lincoln should set the slaves free after he is elected. It would ruin the South. Not everyone is as fortunate as I have been, for there have been many cruelties practiced by slave owners and I'm afraid that if their slaves were ever set free by an emancipation proclamation, they would suffer retribution."

"Let us pray that that will never happen," Keith said soberly. "I don't believe that Lincoln would ever do a drastic thing like that unless he was forced to do it. I believe that he would do everything in his power to avert war or to keep from crippling any part of the nation. He would want to keep the nation undivided."

"If war should come, what would happen to you, Mr. Roland?" Angela asked anxiously.

He regarded her gravely as he said, "I am a graduate of West Point and an officer in the reserve army of the United States, Mistress Angela, even though I am living in the South now. But if war should come and I should be recalled to active duty, I should have to answer that call or else be marked as a deserter."

"Oh dear! How terrible! Then you would be fighting against us when we are friends."

"And very dear friends, I assure you." His eyes swept over both of them but lingered longest on Diana. "Let us hope and pray that that evil day will never come."

"I can say amen to that," Roger said.

When the meal was finished they went back to the living room. Presently the maid brought in coffee and small cakes.

"You have never said so, but you are a believer, are you not?" Roger asked as they sipped the coffee and ate the delicious cookies.

"Yes, I am," Keith replied. "My mother led me to the Lord not long before she died. I have not always been as true to Him as I should have been, perhaps, but I do try to live to please Him. That is why I have had such a predicament about those slaves that I inherited. But you have given me such a helpful solution and I am grateful."

"We would be glad to have you go with us to church, if you would care to," Alicia offered.

"I'd be delighted to go," he said eagerly. "I went when I was in town, but I haven't been since I've been out here. The ride is long and lonely and I just didn't go."

"We manage to get there for the morning service," Roger told him. "It is rather a long trip at night, but we have a vesper service here on the lawn for our people when the weather is good. Come over and help us, if you wish."

"It's a date and thank you for inviting me."

The conversation drifted to other channels until presently Keith rose to go.

"I'm afraid I've stayed longer than I should have," he remarked. "But I've enjoyed myself so much that I forgot about the time."

They went with him to the door and Alicia gave him a cordial invitation to drop in any time he felt like coming.

"We shall be glad to have you come for dinner whenever you wish to," she assured him. "We can always add another plate and you can take pot luck."

"Thank you for making me feel so welcome. I know I shall want to come very often."

When they had reached the door and he was leaving, Diana said, "Would you mind if I walked with you to the gate?"

"I'd be honored," he said gallantly.

They went down the steps together and she waited while he untied his horse and led it by his side as they walked toward the gate.

"I had to take this opportunity to tell you how very sorry I am that I was so rude to you the other morning," she said. "Will you accept my most humble apology?"

Her voice was low and melodious and she was very lovely as she looked appealingly into his eyes while the lamps on the porch cast a dim glow over them.

"Do you need to ask?" he said as she stood close and waited for his answer. "I realize that you were upset and frightened. I assure you that Bruce will never do such a terrible thing again. I shall keep him within bounds."

"I hope that Bruce and I shall be friends some day," she said with a charming smile. "But even though I was frightened and bruised, that was no excuse for such a display of temper. Please believe that I can act decently and I do know how to be polite."

"I believe you."

"Then we can be friends? Real friends?" Her tone was

warm and tender and there was the hint of more then friendship in her glance.

"If that is what you wish," he said.

"Thank you. That makes me very happy."

They had reached the gate and she held out her hand. He took it and bowed over it and pressed his lips to it before he let it go.

"That is the seal of our friendship," he whispered with his face very near her own.

She saw desire in his eyes but she knew that he would control that desire to kiss her, so she withdrew her hand slowly and stepped back a little way as she told him goodnight. He opened the gate and mounted his horse, then waved to her and galloped down the road.

She stood looking after him until the darkness hid him from view, then returned slowly to the house. There was a satisfied little smile upon her lips.

5

ANGELA AND HER MOTHER stood looking after Diana and Keith as they walked down the path. Angela's eyes were serious, but her remark seemed rather flippant.

"She's baiting her hook again. Soon she'll have another sucker landed."

"That doesn't sound like you, Angela," Alicia told her. "You do tease your sister rather unmercifully, but that sounds bitter."

"I'm not bitter, Mother, just sorry and hurt. Why does Diana have to try to make a slave of every man she meets? She doesn't care a thrip for any of them, but she uses every art in her power to make them fall in love with her, then she tries to keep them dangling until she is tired of them. Why is it? How can she get such a thrill out of breaking hearts and disillusioning boys who honor her by falling in love with her?"

"It's because she's never learned the true purpose in life, my child," Alicia said as she put an arm around the girl and they turned back into the house. "She thinks that life was just meant to have a good time in the way she wants it. She won't believe that there is really joy in living for the Lord. I've failed somewhere along the line, but I have tried to teach her that there is no true happiness in life outside of Christ. She is a stubborn little doubter. I only hope that she will not live to regret her refusal to accept Christ as her Saviour."

"If she would only admit it, she would know how happy I am and I don't have a string of admirers hanging around and waiting for a smile. She thinks I'm just a child and that I have no personality because I can't attract every boy I meet. I wouldn't do it if I could. Sometimes I have half a mind to try, just to show her that she isn't the only one with that fatal charm."

"Don't ever think of it, darling," Alicia warned. "That's not the way for a Christian to act. Some day the right man will come along when you are older and you'll be happier with him than she can ever be, the way she is living. She may play around with so many hearts that she will end by having nothing but regret for the broken hearts she has caused."

"Don't worry, Mother. I was only joking. I do wish, though, that she would leave William Mumford alone. He's such a kid and he's so — so — likable, but she has him hypnotized. He forgets that she is older than he is. I know she will break his heart and I can't bear to think of having that happen to him."

Alicia looked at her with a trace of concern.

"Do you care for him, dear?" she asked gently.

Angela colored and hesitated, then said reluctantly, "I like him a lot and I could have fallen in love with him and I think he liked me until she set her eyes upon him and got him on her hook. Now he will scarcely notice me when she is around. It does hurt, but it hurts more to think how she is throwing her life away on such cruel sport. I love her so much and she is so beautiful, but she only loves herself."

Angela kissed her mother goodnight and went to her room. It was still not late and she sat for a while reading from her Bible before she got ready for bed.

Diana came in and saw her in her room reading. She began to undress without saying anything. She dreaded Angela's teasing and she knew that she had laid herself open for it. When she slipped into bed, she lay there thinking over the evening and those few moments at the gate. She was sure that she had wiped out whatever unpleasant memory Keith might have had of her and her heart beat faster as she remembered that look in his eyes. She had been tempted to let him kiss her, but had thought better of it. She was afraid of what he might think of her for allowing such a thing on such a short acquaintance. Later on, when she had him more completely under her spell, she felt that he would not bother about conventions any more than she would when she lured him on to fall a victim to her charms.

Angela finished reading and went to the door of Diana's room. She stood for a moment looking down at her sister while Diana feigned to be asleep, but Angela knew that the girl was only pretending. She could not resist a few words before she prepared for bed.

"I suppose that you and that pesky Yankee are friends at last, since you were thoughtful enough to walk him to the gate. Did he forgive you for letting your temper fly at him when his poor dog barked at you?"

"That's my business, so be quiet and leave me alone." Diana snapped. "I'm sleepy. Go to bed."

"Why can't you let him escape, Diana? He's such a nice person and he's a Christian. Please don't hurt him. I want him for a friend. You have so many others, why not let him be just a friend?"

"If you want him, then take him if you can," Diana replied with a twisted smile as she raised herself on her elbow and faced her sister.

"Perhaps I could if I tried," Angela replied with spirit, "but I wouldn't even try. I don't want him that way. I want to keep him as a friend and he can't be one after you've broken his heart. You never could love him, so why not let him alone?"

"Why not let me alone and mind your own business? You live your life the way you want it and I'm going to live mine the way I want it, so arguing won't get you anywhere."

"You're not only hurting yourself, Diana, honey, but you're hurting Mother. She wants you to live for the Lord and you're getting farther and farther away from Him. You don't even pray before you go to bed like you used to when we were children."

She went to the bed and stroked her sister's cheek.

"I love you so much, Diana. You're so beautiful and you could make such a wonderful Christian. The Lord loves you even more than I do. Why not try to believe that you could be far happier in Him than you ever could be in the world?"

Diana flounced away and turned her back upon her sister.

"Don't bother me! I told you I was sleepy and I don't want to hear any more sermons from you. I get enough of those in the daytime from Mother and you. Go to bed and let me alone."

Angela was silent as she turned away and went to her room, but there were tears in her eyes and upon her cheek as she knelt by her bed and prayed. She prayed as she constantly did, for the sister who seemed utterly devoid of any thought but that of pleasure, the kind of pleasure that could never bring lasting happiness.

The next morning at breakfast Roger's conversation turned to Keith.

"He's a fine young fellow," he remarked. "I feel sorry for him, living there all alone with his memories. I think I'll go over and pay him a little visit this afternoon and see if I can help him in any way about the place. He has a problem on his hands, for it's too late to plant cane and I don't think he has much of a stand. That trustee didn't hurt himself trying to keep things going until Keith got here and the estate was settled."

"What he needs is a wife," Alicia said. "A woman could have that house looking different in no time at all."

"I believe I'll apply for the job," Angela announced.

Her father laughed and asked, "What qualifications do you have to offer, youngster?"

"I can cook and keep house. Mammy Sue has taught me a lot of things that you'd never guess. And I could tell him how very much I like him. I think he'd make an ideal husband. We'd get along famously. I'd even have Bruce making friends with Toby."

"It takes more than liking to make happiness in marriage," her mother said seriously. "Do you think you could fall in love with a man almost ten years older than you are? He thinks you're just a child."

Angela shrugged. "I wasn't thinking of love. I was just feeling sorry for him, because he's so nice and I like him. How long will I have to go on being a child? I'll soon be seventeen and that's getting along in years. Perhaps I could hire myself out to him as his housekeeper. I could at least see that he got enjoyable meals."

"Now you're just being silly," Diana remarked with a curl of her lip.

"How did you like the pesky Yankee?" Roger asked Diana with a twinkle in his eye.

"He'll do," she answered indifferently. "At least unless war breaks out."

"You weren't talking about war at the gate last night, I'm sure."

He chuckled as she gave him an indignant look and colored self-consciously.

"I was only trying to do what I thought you would want me to do," she replied. "I asked his pardon for being so rude when my horse threw me."

"What a dutiful daughter my sister is becoming," Angela remarked. Then as Diana flashed an angry glance at her, she giggled and became very much interested in her cereal.

"Suppose we talk of something else," Alicia suggested.

When Sunday morning came Angela was surprised to see Diana already in the dining room for their early morning breakfast, dressed and ready for church. She had on one of her most charming dresses, a pale yellow with sprigs of blue flowers scattered over its shimmering surface. She looked lovely and demure, with her hair parted at the side and a row of ringlets across her forehead, while curls fell over her shoulder from the comb which held them in place at the nape of her neck.

"Why Sis, how lovely you look!" Angela cried as she came into the dining room a few minutes later. "Don't tell me that you're going to church with us today."

"You talk as if I never go," Diana remarked with a frown.

"Oh yes, you go sometimes, but those times are few and far between. I don't know who will be the happiest to have you go today, Mother or Mr. Roland."

Diana turned upon her angrily and cried in low tones so that her parents could not hear, for they were coming down the stairs just then, "You leave him out of this, do you hear? I'm tired of your everlasting teasing and I don't intend to take any more of it, so stop it!"

"I'm sorry, Diana," Angela said humbly. "I didn't mean to make you angry. I do try not to tease, but somehow it just seems to bubble up and come out when I least expect it. I'm really glad that you're going with us and I promise to behave. Cross my heart," she added with a smile.

She bent over and kissed her sister on her cheek and Diana, somewhat mollified, took her place at the table when her parents came in and sat down.

"Well, well! You're dressed as if you were going somewhere," Roger remarked to Diana when he had given thanks and the maid was bringing in the breakfast. "Could it be that you are honoring us with your presence at church this morning?"

"Isn't that what you want me to do?" she asked, beginning to feel uncomfortable.

"I wonder if you're going just to please me, or because

we'll have company this morning going with us?" He gave her an amused smile.

"Oh, Father," she cried as a frown brought her dark brows together. "If you start that I shall stay at home. I do go occasionally, and you know it. Does it call for all of this excitement just because I chose to go today? First Angela and now you. Why don't you add your bit, Mother?"

"I will," Alicia said firmly. "Eat your breakfast and don't get so angry whenever someone tries to have a little fun and tease you a little."

"A little!" she scoffed. "I've had nothing else from Angela for days."

"She meant no harm and you know it, so do try to be agreeable at least until we finish eating. Mr. Roland will be here shortly and we'll have to be leaving."

During the rest of the meal Diana was grimly silent while Angela and her father kept up a patter of small talk.

Presently Keith arrived and they were ready to leave for the city. He looked very handsome, with his slim figure encased in tight-fitting gray trousers and long-tailed black coat, while a tall silk hat covered his thick brown hair.

"We'll let you sit in front with Roger," Alicia said. "I'll sit in the back with the girls."

Diana tried to hide her disappointment. She had hoped that Keith would be allowed to sit with them. Alicia smiled to herself as she saw the expression upon Diana's face.

The road leading to the city passed plantations stretched along the way until they came to the little village of Carrollton, just outside the city. The two horses made good time and they were well ahead of time when they at last reached Canal Street where the horses' hoofs struck sparks from the cobblestones as they trotted along toward the church farther down the street. The city was quiet on this spring morning and only those on their way to church seemed to be stirring. There were several vehicles tied in front of the church when they arrived and friends came up to greet them as they got out and joined those going toward the entrance.

Angela saw young William Mumford coming toward them and her heart beat a little faster as she watched him approaching. They had been friends at school and had had a childish romance when they were younger. But when he grew older, William had forgotten that romance while he hovered about Diana, fascinated by her beauty and her power to charm.

Angela waved to him, but her eyes clouded and her spirits drooped as she let her hand fall to her side, for she saw that he was not looking at her. He didn't seem to be aware that she was even there. He had eyes only for Diana.

As he came nearer, what he felt for her glowed unmistakably in his deep blue eyes.

"It seems ages since I saw you," he exclaimed as he made his way to Diana and took the hand that she held out to him. "I wasn't hoping to see you here today, but I came anyway thinking that you just might come. May I sit by you in the service?"

She gave him a ravishing smile and said in cordial tones, "If you wish. I don't believe you know our guest this morning. Mr. Roland, allow me to present Mr. William Mumford, an old friend of the family."

The two acknowledged the introduction while the boy's eyes scanned Keith's tall figure with jealous appraisal. Diana turned to Keith.

"You will sit with us, I'm sure," she remarked as she gave him a smile.

"You already have company," he told her, "so I'll sit with Mistress Angela, if she is willing."

For an instant her smile disappeared and a glint crept into her eyes which made them seem hard and cold, then she managed the smile again, but not before he had seen the change and surmised the cause.

"I have two sides, haven't I?" she asked archly. "I shall be honored to have you sit beside me."

He smiled and turned to Angela. "What do you say?" he asked. "I have two sides also, so will you give me the honor of sitting on my other side?"

Angela giggled. "I'd be pleased as Punch, sir."

She followed them demurely as they entered the church.

During this little scene William had not once even glanced at Angela. He was too much worried over the presence of this new rival. Just another one to make it more difficult for him to make any progress in his effort to win Diana's heart. He was not aware that he had not even spoken to Angela. The girl's heart was heavy, but she wore a bright smile as they entered the church and took their places in the pew just behind her parents.

She shared the hymnal with Keith, much to Diana's chagrin, for she was forced to share hers with William, but she gave William a smile which brought joy to his heart while he burst forth into song as they began the hymn. His hand touched hers as they held the book and his heart beat faster as she let it lay against his. She knew how to play the coquette's game like the expert she was, for, though she would be doing all in her power to captivate Keith, she was not willing to let another of her victims grow cold, so she hid her disappointment and made the best of the situation.

The sermon was powerful and carried a message of salvation through the blood atonement which was made possible on the Cross of Calvary. Angela prayed earnestly that somehow her sister's heart would be touched and that she would yield her life to the Lord, but Diana had other things upon her mind and she did not hear half the preacher said.

When the service was over and they left the church, William lingered at Diana's side. She was impatient for him to leave so that she could devote her attention to Keith who had not even looked at her once during the service, but the boy would not leave.

"How soon may I come out to see you?" he asked as they went toward their carriage.

"Give us a little more time to get settled," she advised. "It won't be long before we'll be having you and the others out for some fun. Perhaps I'll be seeing you again next Sunday."

"I hope so," he murmured fervently as they reached the carriage and he was forced to leave.

On the way home the two men on the front seat kept a continual flow of conversation, but the three on the back seat were unusually silent. There were disturbing thoughts in the mind of each. Diana was peeved because Keith had displayed so little interest in her. She knew that it was because William had come into the picture and spoiled everything. She wished that she had dismissed the boy at once, but she could not have done that without showing Keith how rude she was and she could not afford to have that happen.

Angela was still crushed and heavy of heart because William had ignored her so completely. She hoped that no one noticed. Perhaps it was because he was jealous of Keith. But why did Diana have to take this one boy from her? She felt that he had belonged to her, for they had so much in common, but now they had nothing and she had only a young girl's blasted dreams and hopes.

Alicia was worried more than ever over Diana. She was proud of this beautiful child of hers, yet she grieved because she was so worldly and blind and deaf to the Gospel. She feared for her, of what the future would bring to her if she pursued the course she had started upon. She had witnessed that little scene at the church and she had seen how hurt Angela was and how bravely she had tried to hide the hurt under her smile and it grieved her because of this and the knowledge that Diana was the cause of that hurt and that she was so self-centered that she did not even care what her sister might feel.

She knew that Diana had deliberately taken the boy's affection for Angela and that she gloated over the knowledge instead of being sorry that she had hurt her sister. Where would it all end, Alicia wondered. Only the Lord knew and she prayed that He would save the child she loved, who was on the way to sorrow and ruin if she did not change her course and receive Christ as her Saviour.

6

KEITH WAS INVITED TO STAY for dinner and he accepted the cordial invitation with pleasure. It was lonesome in his big old house and the thought of the tempting food and the companionship was more than he could resist.

Today the meal was even more lavish than the previous dinner had been. There was a roast which was tender and succulent and also a baked ham. Potatoes were whipped to a frothy mound while fresh garden vegetables added variety to the meal. Pickles and jellies were served in cut glass dishes while hot rolls were passed at frequent intervals.

"We always have a cold lunch on Sunday evening, so as to give the kitchen help an afternoon off," Roger explained. "Then there will be no excuse for them not to attend vespers at sundown. If you will stay for the service, we would love to have you and you can take pot luck with us afterwards. I'm sure the girls will be pleased to have you. How about it, girls?"

"We'd love it," Angela exclaimed. "When you and Mother go upstairs for your afternoon nap, then perhaps we'll get a chance to have a few words with Mr. Roland. We never do when you two are around."

They all laughed while Diana remained silent. Roger turned to her and repeated his question.

"What have you to say, my dear?"

"We'd be glad to have you, Mr. Roland." She gave him a smile. "Sunday afternoon is very dull but I know it will not be dull if you are here."

"Thank you," Keith replied with an answering smile. "With such an invitation, I couldn't say no if I wanted to and I'm sure that I have no desire to say no."

When the meal was finished, they went into the room across the hall. It was a combination of living room and library. In one corner of the room near the window there was a mahogany secretary with the shelves above the desk filled with books while along the wall were more shelves lined with books. At one end of the room there was a large marble mantle with a bronze clock ticking softly. On each side of the clock was a Dresden figurine.

There were comfortable cushioned chairs and a lounge near a window. Just beneath the open window roses grew in profusion and their fragrance drifted into the room, mingling with the more pungent perfume of the honeysuckle growing upon a lattice at the side of the house. The floor was covered with a thick carpet of dull blue with roses scattered over its surface while the draperies matched it in color.

"What a charming room," Keith remarked as Roger led the way and invited him to a deep cushioned chair. "It reminds me of what my old home used to look like before it was left to become shabby and neglected. I hope to restore it one day to what it used to be."

"What it needs is a woman's touch," Roger said.

Diana looked startled and gave him a warning glance and he realized that he had made a blunder.

Angela giggled, relieving the situation.

"Father! You wouldn't be hinting to Mr. Roland that he might find that woman's touch here, would you? You've put him on the spot."

Roger laughed and Keith smiled.

"It did sound that way, didn't it, but I assure you, Mr. Roland, that I had no such thought. I'm not anxious to be rid of my girls, and I'm sure that they have no designs upon you —not at present, at least," he added with a chuckle.

"Oh, but I have," Angela retorted with a michievous glance at her father. "We were talking about you, Mr. Roland, about how lonesome you must be, there all alone, and Father made that same remark, about how lonesome you must be and that you needed a woman's touch about the house. Or perhaps it was Mother who said it. At any rate, I said I would offer my services as your housekeeper, but they didn't think that was such a good idea."

"You're simply irrepressible," her father remarked as he looked at her and shook his head.

"Perhaps you already have someone in mind to give that woman's touch," Angela suggested. "Someone you left behind when you came here."

"No, I have no one in mind," he told her. "There were only a few friends of my parents and their children with whom I was acquainted. I didn't have much time for romance. When I finished school and got my appointment to West Point and then served my time in the army, I was away from home most of the time. It has been only a short time since I finished my service, between my homecoming and the death of my father. I have not had time to think of anything but business affairs."

They talked for a while longer, discussing the sermon of the morning, then turning to politics and the growing war clouds that seemed to be hovering nearer. Then Roger and Alicia excused themselves leaving the young people together.

"I heard you singing this morning and I know that you have a good voice," Angela told Keith. "Would you mind singing some hymns or would you rather just relax and talk?"

"Don't you think that Mr. Roland will get enough of singing later on at the vesper service?" Diana asked.

"I love to sing," he told her, "and if you would like to, I would enjoy singing some of the old hymns that I love. I haven't had the opportunity to sing them for some time. Which one of you plays?"

"We both do," Angela told him, "but Diana prefers classical music while I like to play hymns. She has the talent. I just try to play. She can sing better than I can, so I'll let you two sing while I play and listen."

She went to the piano and began to play one of the old hymns, "Amazing Grace," softly and reverently.

"For goodness' sake, play something with more life in it than that," Diana exclaimed.

"That is one of my favorites," Keith told her. "Let's sing a verse or two if you don't mind."

Diana's voice, a contralto, was quite good and it blended

well with Keith's. He remarked about it when they had finished the first verse and she was in a much more amiable mood after his compliment.

"I love this last verse, for it has such promise," he remarked. " 'When we've been there ten thousand years, bright shining as the sun, We've no less days to sing God's praise than when we've first begun.' The Christian has such a wonderful future ahead of him. I can't understand why, with such a glorious future to look forward to, everyone doesn't accept the gift of salvation and live for that day."

"Perhaps they feel that there is much in this life to enjoy, so why live a life of self-denial now when that future life is so very far away?" Diana remarked while Angela's fingers wandered idly over the keys.

Angela had more talent than she professed to have and Keith saw that she played with deep feeling, as if her whole heart was in the theme of the hymn. Diana, on the other hand, sang mechanically, even though her voice was sweet and melodious.

Keith regarded her thoughtfully before he answered, then he said, "Being a Christian and looking forward to what is in store in the future, does not mean that we can't enjoy life while we are living and waiting for that time to come. Only a Christian can have real joy. If self-denial is necessary, it too can be a joy if one is only surrendered to God."

"I suppose it all depends upon how we look at life," she replied.

"It all depends upon what we have in our heart that determines the way we look at life," he told her. "To the person without salvation, life is just the gratification of selfish desires, but to the one who has the love of God in his heart, life is a yielded one and the only true joy is found in living it the way God directs us to live it. Only then is there real and lasting peace in the heart, because that person knows that there is nothing between his soul and his Lord."

"You would make a good preacher," Diana remarked.

"That's what I wanted to be instead of being a soldier," he said, "but my father willed it otherwise and I became a soldier to please him, but I've never been happy about it. One day I hope to be able to give out the Gospel, if not from the pulpit, then perhaps on some mission field."

"How wonderful that would be!" Angela exclaimed. "You could never desire anything better than to win souls for the Lord."

She began to play another hymn and they sang it together, much to Diana's relief. She wasn't enjoying this turn of the conversation. She felt that Keith suspected that she was not a Christian and she was afraid that he would think less of her because of it. However, she had seen his eyes fixed upon her when he thought she was not looking and she knew that he admired her beauty, even if he did not agree with her in spiritual matters. She did not like the thought that he might become a minister of the Gospel. That prospect was decidedly unpleasant, but then, that was a hope for the future which might never be realized. In the meantime much could happen to change his mind.

Angela turned to him with a sudden inspiration when they had finished the song.

"Why not talk to the slaves this evening? Father tries to talk to them after he reads from the Bible, but I'm sure that he would be glad to have you take his place. They hear him all the time and they would enjoy hearing someone else."

"I don't know about that," Keith replied. "We'd better wait and see what your father has to say. I'd be willing to try, if he wants me to."

"We'll ask him when he comes down."

When Roger and Alicia came down later, Angela told her father what she had suggested to Keith. He was delighted and asked Keith if he would take his place.

"I'll do my best," he said and so it was agreed.

When the sun was almost down the Negroes began to gather on the lawn at the back of the house. They sat upon the grass with the children about them and waited for Roger and the others to come from the house. Two of the men carried a little reed organ out and placed it nearby and Angela took her place before it and began to play softly a hymn that they loved. They began to hum the tune, then presently their voices rose louder as they began to sing. Their natural ability to harmonize was given full expression and the song took on a new meaning to Keith as he listened to a harmony that he had never heard before. It was beautiful and his heart was stirred as he saw the expression on some of the dark faces. He knew from the rapt look upon them as their bodies swayed to the rhythm of the music, that they were believers and he knew that Roger had done more than being just a kind master. He had been a real evangel to the people under his care.

When the singing had ended, Roger introduced Keith as their new neighbor and then turned the service over to him. Keith did not talk long, but what he said seemed to strike a responsive chord in the hearts of many in his audience, for they responded with loud amens and "Praise de Lawd." He gave them a few simple words of explanation of the passage he had read and then gave them his testimony, how the Lord had changed his whole outlook on life and had given him a new purpose in life, to live only for the Lord and what He would have him do. Then he pictured to them briefly what was in store for them in the future, when the Lord should return and when His faithful ones would receive rewards according to what they had done for Him.

When he reached the climax of his message, there were shouts from many throats, while tears coursed down many a black cheek. When he ended with a short prayer, they gathered about him with simple words of appreciation. Keith was touched by the words and also by the freedom which they exercised. It seemed unusual to him, for he had never realized that there could be such freedom in slavery. It was a new and thrilling experience to him. He remarked about it as they returned to the house for lunch.

"If all slave owners treated their slaves as you treat yours, sir, there would never have been any question of emancipation. They are as happy as if they were free."

"They are free," Roger reminded him. "Because they know

that I care for them, they do not take advantage of me because I allow them so much freedom. I have never had a single one of them to make me sorry that I have treated them as a Christian should."

"Unfortunately those in the North have seen only the worst side of the picture."

"Unfortunately the worst is too often the picture," Roger replied sadly. "All slavery is terrible and I feel that it is a sin in the sight of God, but so many slave owners have no feeling for their slaves. They either leave them to cruel overseers or they treat them cruelly themselves. The greatest cruelty I know of is that of separating families and wrecking so many lives. I can't blame the North for wanting to see an end of a condition that makes this possible, but there are right and wrong ways of ending this cruel institution. The North should remember that when slavery was first introduced in our land, they became slave owners as well as we in the South, but because they found that it was not beneficial to them, they let the South take over. Now they want slavery abolished without due recompense to the owners of slaves and that, as I said before, would ruin the South. I am for abolition, but in a fair way that would give the owners of slaves time to adjust themselves financially to the new order. I would heartily agree to a law like that."

"I thoroughly agree with you," Keith replied.

Angela restrained a desire to tease Diana for being so interested in the vesper service. She never attended. This evening, however, she was not only there, but she joined in the singing as if she really enjoyed it and when Keith gave his talk, there was not a more interested listener.

When Keith was ready to leave he turned to the two girls.

"Would you like an early morning horseback ride if the weather is good tomorrow morning?"

Diana spoke up before Angela had time to answer.

"Angela likes to sleep late, but I'd be happy to go. I love to ride in the early morning and it is rather lonely, riding alone."

Angela said nothing, but her wide accusing eyes rested upon her sister. Diana refused to look at her. They were out in the hall and Roger and Alicia did not hear them.

They named the time and Keith said he would be waiting for her at the gate. When he had left Angela turned upon Diana.

"Why did you have to lie to him?" she demanded. "You know that I love to get up early and ride. I would have been with you the other morning if you hadn't slipped out so much earlier than usual. I would have loved to go with you two."

"There's no need for you to be so angry," Diana retorted coolly. "I've got to have a little time with Mr. Roland away from Mother and Father so that I can have a chance to make him understand how sorry I am for the way I acted the other morning."

"I thought you settled that little matter at the gate the other night," Angela retorted.

"Not to my satisfaction. But don't be so upset. You can go with us some other time. I just want to be alone with him this one time."

"Some other time! After you've told him that I like to sleep late. I'd either have to let him know that you were lying or else have him think that I was running after him by tagging along with you."

"Wouldn't that be what you would be doing?" Diana asked with a twisted smile.

"You know it wouldn't," Angela retorted heatedly. "All I want is his friendship. But you don't even want me to have that. I have no designs upon him."

"What makes you think that I have any?" Diana demanded. "Perhaps all I want is his friendship."

"Friendship! You'd never be satisfied to have such a good looking man just for your friend. You want to make a slave of him like you have all the others. How can you be so heartless?"

Diana smiled mockingly as she said, "I'm not heartless,

darling. I just have a large heart, something you can't understand."

"I understand only too well and I fear for you, Diana," Angela replied as she left her and went upstairs.

7

DIANA SEEMED TO HAVE TAKEN on an entirely new personality when she and Keith rode out together the next morning. She looked particularly lovely in a light blue riding habit with a dark blue hat perched upon her black curls, with the inevitable white feather draped over the side. Her eyes were brilliant and the color was high in her face, emphasizing the beauty of her flawless complexion. Keith did not try to hide his admiration, though he did not waste time in silly compliments.

They rode slowly for a while, then Diana suggested a race. She was not only in high spirits, but she was eager to show her skill as a rider. They raced for some distance, then drew rein as he came up behind her.

"You let me win on purpose," she chided.

He smiled. "Suppose we just admit that your horse was faster than mine. May I say that you are an expert rider? You ride as well as any man and much more gracefully."

"Thank you," and she gave him a bright smile. "Riding is the one thing I pride myself on. I love it and I do want to excell in this one thing at least. I've done a little target shooting and a little rowing, for I love all sports, but I'm not proficient in anything else."

She was gay and entertaining, keeping up a flow of conversation that surprised and delighted him. He had feared that she would be dull and quiet, for she had talked so little in the few times they had been together. He remarked about it when they had stopped under the shade of some trees to let their horses rest for a while.

"You seem like a different person this morning," he said. "You've been so quiet and reserved and seemed so aloof before. Today you're full of sparkle and very charming and entertaining. I'm agreeably surprised."

"I suppose I did seem a very dull person, but the reason is quite simple. I don't ever seem to say the right thing when I'm with my sister or my parents. Angela is the perfect child and never displeases them by what she says or does, but I am the black sheep of the family. They disapprove of me because I don't think as they do about spiritual matters. I know that I grieve them, but I can't help it if I have my own beliefs which do not agree with theirs."

"You mean that you grieve them because you're not a Christian." He spoke plainly and seriously.

Her anger flared and she answered rather caustically, "I am not a heathen, Mr. Roland. I believe in God."

"So do the devils," he replied, smiling slightly.

"What do you mean by that?" she asked crisply.

"Jesus said that they believe and tremble because they know that their future will be eternal punishment. Believing in God has to be more than head knowledge. You have to believe in your heart to become a true Christian. But then, I'm sure that you know that. You have been reared in a Christian home, so you must know the way of salvation, even though you do not choose to accept it for your life."

"I'm not willing to give up all that I enjoy in life just to live like my parents think I should. It is all right for them to live quietly, for they have had their good times. I don't see why I should be deprived of mine when I'm still so young. All of life is before me and I feel that there is plenty of time for me to settle down and become a Christian when I'm older and have had my fun."

"Is that the way your sister feels about it? I'm sure that she is a Christian in the true sense of the word, yet she seems to be bubbling over with the joy of living. She seems very happy. I don't believe she feels that she has given up any of the good things of life, the things that really count."

"Angela is still just a child even though she is almost seventeen. She still enjoys feeding the pigs and chickens, training her colt, and playing with her dog. She doesn't even know what real fun is."

"I believe she does," he argued. "I think she has found the source of real joy. She gets as much fun out of doing the things she does as you do following your search for happiness."

"I'm not searching for happiness, Mr. Roland. I am enjoying it," she informed him loftily. "Perhaps some day I shall change my viewpoint when I'm older and can settle down to quiet living and then perhaps I shall please my father by becoming the kind of a Christian he wants me to become."

"I wonder if you realize that we can't become a Christian just whenever we decide to become one," he said gravely. "We can only come to the Lord when His Spirit draws us, not just when we decide to. God has issued a warning to us that His Spirit will not always strive with us. Jesus said that 'no man can come to me unless my Father draw him.' I would hate to think that the time might come to you when you would discover that it was too late and that you had heard the Spirit's pleading for the last time. Hadn't you better think about it for fear that that time might come when it would be too late for you?"

Her serious eyes met his for a moment, then she smiled engagingly and said, "In the words of Agrippa, 'Almost thou persuadest me to be a Christian.'"

"Then let me repeat the words of the apostle Paul, 'I would to God that you were almost and altogether such as I am.'"

"Does it really make any difference to you?" she asked in low tones, while into her eyes there crept a warm, tender, appealing light.

He was on his guard as he met her gaze and heard the tone of her voice. Her beauty was a powerful force and he had caught just a glimpse of how she was using that beauty to allure. He had observed her dealing with young William Mumford.

"It makes a great deal of difference to me," he said slowly. "I realize what you could be if you were surrendered to the Lord. Your sister has everything, youth, beauty, and the one thing that is the most precious of all, the gift of salvation. You are even more beautiful and you have a charm that is alluring when you choose to exert it, but you lack the one thing that would make you almost perfect."

She gave him a look which only she could manage. She was the perfect actress and she knew how to use her eyes and the tones of her voice. Her look was like that of a child asking for help, yet it held something that no child could ever know.

"Would it make you like me just a little better if I should have that one thing?" As he hesitated, measuring that look and the tone of her voice, she continued. "I do want your friendship very, very much. You're so different from all the others. All the boys I know are so immature and they are worldly just like me. If you could be my friend, perhaps I should want what you have and perhaps I would accept what you have accepted before it is too late."

He wondered how much of coquetry there was and how much sincerity in her words and in her attitude, but he answered her truthfully.

"I do want to be your friend, Diana. You'll let me call you that, won't you?"

"Of course."

"Then call me Keith." His warm smile broke forth again. "Let that be the seal of our friendship."

"Will you try to teach me more about what you have? I will try to be a receptive pupil."

"It isn't a matter of teaching, as I'm sure you know. It's a matter of just yielding. I believe you already know the way, the truth, and the necessity for obedience to the truth, but I am willing to do anything that will make you yield to the Lord and become one of His."

"Thank you. I promise to try to be obedient. Would you join us for breakfast?" she invited, changing the subject abruptly.

"That would be imposing, so I'd better not accept, but I shall be dropping in often, if you will let me."

"You will be most welcome any time you come," she assured him while they rode out once more upon the road and returned home slowly.

She was more subdued, but she was still charming and talkative and he was falling under the spell of her beauty even though he knew that it was not wise. When she left him at the gate with the invitation to come to see them soon, he rode home slowly. The house seemed more empty than ever as he gave his horse to the boy who came at his summons and went in to breakfast.

What Roger had said was true, he said to himself as he sat down to his lonely meal. He needed a woman's touch and a woman's presence to take away this loneliness and make his house a real home. But how could he ask any woman to marry him when times were so uncertain? If war should come he would be called away and might never return. Even if war should not come, how could he ask any woman to share what might be his poverty? If this plantation did not prove profitable, he would have nothing to offer any woman. Besides, who was there whom he might ask to become his wife?

Diana's face rose before him, with her dark beauty and the almost hypnotic allure that her beauty held. As he looked at her through the eyes of memory, he shook his head. She was not a Christian and she would bring only sorrow and heartache to any man who married her. She would never be satisfied to be tied down to one man for life. Even so, she was not for him. He sighed deeply as he bowed his head and gave thanks before he began to eat.

8

Diana came in to breakfast a few minutes late, but this time she did not come in like a storm cloud. She was radiant and exuberant and greeted everyone with a smile instead of the usual casual good morning.

"You must have had a pleasant ride with our friend," her father remarked with a knowing wink at his wife.

"Yes, we did have a good time. We had a race and I beat him, but I think he just let me beat him. He is really quite nice."

She glanced at Angela, expecting a teasing remark from her, but her sister was silent and she was not even looking at Diana. She seemed intent upon her cereal. Diana felt guilty and tried to make amends.

"Mr. Roland wanted to know if you would go with us next time. I told him you loved to ride."

"That was very thoughtful of you," Angela replied without looking at her.

Diana detected the note of sarcasm in Angela's voice, but she ignored it and turned her attention to her father. She was more talkative than usual. Roger responded to her effort at conversation while he guessed the reason for her high spirits. He could not refrain from remarking about it.

"Evidently you convinced Mr. Roland that you could be a charming young lady instead of a hot-tempered, ill-mannered one."

"He didn't say and I didn't ask him," she said as some of the effervescence left her. "We had other things to talk about."

"Politics perhaps?" His eyes twinkled.

"No. Religion," she flashed, bringing a surprised look to his eyes.

"Dear me!" he exclaimed. "What a serious subject for an early morning ride."

"I found it quite interesting." She smiled to herself at his look of surprise. "He makes religion a most interesting subject."

"I can understand that," Angela volunteered.

Diana gave her a withering look and turned the conversation to another subject.

"When are we going to have a barbecue for the folks in town? Mr. Roland said he had never been to a real Southern barbecue."

"Then we shall have to let him see what one is like," Roger said. "I'll arrange for one before long."

Acting upon the cordial invitation to come over often, Keith came over a few evenings later and sat for some time with the family. They played several games and sang a few songs before he left. He suggested another ride with Diana and when she accepted his invitation she told him that perhaps she could persuade Angela to go with them. Angela interrupted before Keith could answer.

"I believe you made it clear to Mr. Roland that I love to sleep late, so please don't expect me to go with you. Thank you so very much for thinking of asking me."

Keith was puzzled by the hurt look in her eyes and by the serious tone of her voice. She had been unusually quiet all evening and he sensed that there was something wrong and wondered about it.

During the weeks that followed he was a frequent visitor at the house, coming sometimes, at their insistence, for a meal, but at other times spending the evening with the family. They dropped their formality at his request and called him Keith, while he addressed the girls by their given names.

True to his promise, Roger planned a barbecue for his friends in town. Long tables were set under the trees on one side of the house, while the slaves prepared the food in the barbecue pit some distance behind the house. There were chickens and a young pig on spits over the fire while one of the slaves turned them slowly until they were cooked and browned to perfection.

The guests began to arrive early and before long the lawn and the wide porch was a buzzing hive of chatter and laughter. Diana was in her glory, for she was surrounded by a number of her admirers.

This was a novel experience for Keith and he enjoyed meeting new people and his old friends, for the Mayhews were there with Dot. He saw that Diana was the center of attention among the boys and he observed more than one girl's jealous eyes watching as her escort hovered around Diana while she herself was left to talk with the other girls who had been likewise abandoned. He looked on with amusement, watching Diana as she sparkled and entertained the group which surrounded her. She cast an occasional glance in his direction, but he did not respond to the invitation in her eyes to come over and join them.

He understood what she meant when she had said that she wanted to get the most out of life while she was still young. This was what she called getting the most out of life, basking in the admiration of young fellows whose hearts she might break and enjoy it while they were being broken. It grieved him and he felt sorry for her. He had no desire to become a member of her court, yet he could understand why the others could not stay away. She was perhaps not only the most beautiful girl he had ever seen, but there was a magnetic charm about her that drew men in spite of themselves. She could be entertaining as well as charming, as was evidenced by the laughter that frequently followed some remark of hers. He felt the lure of her beauty even while he was judging her and speculating upon her motives and knowing how wrong they were, of how little benefit to anyone but herself and the satisfying of her vanity.

He sauntered over to where the group of neglected girls were sitting together talking and pretending not to care that they had been left to themselves, deserted by their escorts. Angela was watching young Mumford and her heart ached for him, for she could see the look of desperation in his eyes and upon his face as he tried to get a word with Diana. He had scarcely spoken to her, for he had been so eager to get to Diana before the others arrived. He had had only a few moments with Diana until the others came and surrounded her.

"I wonder if I could join this feminine aggregation," Keith asked as he approached them.

"Perhaps you could console us for being neglected," Angela said with mock sadness. "Isn't it a pity that we can't attract even one man?"

Dot giggled and retorted, "We've attracted the best looking one of them all, haven't we?"

"Did we attract him or is he just feeling sorry for us?" Angela asked, pulling a long face. "But what is one lone man among so many girls? We might begin pulling hair over him at any moment, since we're so desperate and forlorn."

"You'll never be forlorn nor be desperate for attention," Keith remarked laughing, while the others joined in the laughter. "Not as long as you have that sense of humor and are as lovely as you are. Just give yourself a little time and you'll be like a flower with the bees buzzing around it."

"How nice of you to say that," Angela replied with a smile. "I'm afraid that time will never come until Diana decides which one of her admirers she wants and gets married and out of the way. What chance do any of us have as long as she is single? We'll all have to wish for an early marriage for her."

They giggled again. They were in the humor by now to giggle at anything and they began to chatter at a lively pace with Keith who was enjoying their exuberance, even though much of it might be quite silly and juvenile. He felt ages older than they were, but he enjoyed them just the same. It had been so long since he had been to a party. In fact parties had been very few in his life, and for the time being he forgot his loneliness.

Diana had been watching him even while she was entertaining the group about her. She was disappointed that he did not come over and join them and she could not stand it any longer to see him enjoying himself without being with her.

She sauntered over to where they were, followed by the boys, including young Mumford.

"I wonder if you have met all these friends," she said to Keith. "Allow me to introduce them."

He had met most of them, but he acknowledged the introduction of the others. Angela's eyes flashed fire, but she said nothing. It was plain to her why Diana had interrupted their fun. She couldn't bear to see Keith having fun away from her. He was the only one who had not been hooked, as Angela expressed it. She wondered if Keith saw Diana's motive in interrupting them.

Keith saw and he understood and he smiled to himself. Even the most stupid could have seen.

"Won't you join us at our table?" Diana invited. "We're almost ready to eat."

"I'm afraid your table will be crowded, even without me," he countered. "How about letting me sit with Angela and Dot wherever they sit?"

Angela had difficulty to keep from laughing at the sudden change of expression upon Diana's face. She couldn't have looked more surprised if Keith had struck her. She had never met with such a refusal and for an instant she was speechless, but she regained her poise in a moment.

"Just as you wish, Mr. Roland," she replied in her most formal tone. She turned to the group about her. "Suppose we go back and continue our little argument."

She turned and left while the boys trailed behind her, scarcely giving a glance to the girls they had brought. Angela gave Keith a smile, a very wise little smile which told him that she understood.

"Thank you for honoring us with your company, Mr. Roland," she said, imitating Diana's voice and manner. "Dot and I and these other neglected girls will enjoy having you at our table."

He gave her an amused smile as dinner was announced and they took their places about the long tables. The elders were grouped together at one table. Keith thought he had never seen so much food displayed at one time. The aroma of barbecued meat filled the air invitingly, while the array of tempting platters made him drool, as he remarked to Angela. There were jellies and preserved figs and plums, homemade pickles and relishes in cut glass bowls, cakes that looked as if they would melt in one's mouth, covered with creamy icing. Tall glasses were filled with iced fruit juices instead of the customary wine usually served at most of the picnic dinners and barbecues. Roger did not drink intoxicating liquors and he never served wine.

Keith wondered how these people could possibly be expected to consume all this food, but when he mentioned it to Angela she told him that when they were finished, the slaves in the quarters would have a feast themselves. He was touched by this further evidence of Roger's thought for his slaves. He wished some of his Northern friends who believed only the worst about slave owners could know Roger and see this plantation and how the slaves were treated.

Before they began to eat Roger offered thanks and then the chatter began again while everyone ate and enjoyed the delicious food.

When the meal was finished some of the older people gathered on the porch and talked while others set up wickets for a game of croquet. The young people wandered away under the trees. Diana managed with cleverness which amazed Keith, to separate him from the other girls and to lead him with her hand upon his arm away from the crowd toward a bench in the far corner of the garden. He scarcely realized how she managed it, but here he was, away from the swarm of other boys who had gone meekly back to their partners. He was her captive for the time being, whether he wished it or not. He marveled at her ingenuity and her persistence while he fell once more under the spell of her beauty. She was very lovely in her dress of pale pink, with a ruffled skirt billowing from her slim waist. There was a black velvet ribbon about her throat, with a little diamond encrusted heart dangling from it against her white petal-like skin. Her dark eyes were brilliant under the curling lashes for she was in her element today and she was glowing and sparkling with her idea of the joy of living.

When they were seated she cast a sympathetic glance upon him as she remarked, "I'm sure you were bored to death with those silly girls, but it was sweet of you to be nice to them."

"On the contrary, I was enjoying myself," he replied. "They were bubbling over and their humor was most refreshing. While I was listening to them and being entertained in a most unusual way, I was witnessing something that was quite revealing."

His smile was enigmatic and it puzzled her.

"What was that?" she asked.

"I was very much interested in watching some poor moths fluttering in the light of a brilliant candle flame, or perhaps I should use another metaphor which may be even worse, wearing themselves out trying to reach a star whose lovely brilliant light drew them on to possible destruction."

As she listened, with her wide eyes fastened upon his face, the smile left her lips and her eyes lost their brilliant luster and grew cold.

"How do you do it, and why?" He shook his head and his eyes were serious.

"I'm afraid I don't understand you, Mr. Roland," she said frigidly.

"Don't be angry, my dear Diana, and don't call me Mr. Roland, because when you do that I know that I have displeased you and I don't want to do that. I want us to be friends, always and forever, no matter what may happen. But how can you get any pleasure out of taking every girl's boy friend away from her and keeping him hanging upon your smile?"

"I don't take them away," she informed him stiffly, while her eyes held a spark of anger. "Could I help it if they came to pay their respects to me and when I was cordial to them, they just stayed on? Could I be rude enough to send them away?"

"You could have dismissed them without being rude, but you didn't want to. You wanted to keep everyone of them hovering about you, no matter how their friends might feel at being neglected."

"Could I help it if they preferred me?" she retorted with a toss of her head.

"Yes, you could help it," he told her seriously. "You did everything in your power to make them prefer you. You have an amazing beauty and an amazing knowledge of how to use that beauty and you use it to lure men and to break their hearts. And you don't seem to care how much you might hurt them."

"It is quite apparent that I shall never break your heart," she remarked.

Her eyes were dark and the glow had left them. This conversation was far different from what she had anticipated and what she had planned.

"I pray that you never shall," he said fervently.

"It is also quite apparent that you don't approve of me." Her voice was bitter, but he fancied that he detected a note of disappointment in it. He knew very well why she had inveigled him into coming here with her. She was hoping to "bait her hook for another sucker," as Angela has so graphically put it. But he was interested in something far different from what she had on her mind. He was interested in her soul, something which she seemed to have forgotten, in spite of what she had said that morning on their first ride.

"Why do you do it, Diana, my dear?" he asked as he took her hand and held it. "You said not long ago that you wanted to learn more about salvation from me, yet I fear that desire has left you in your pursuit of men's hearts."

She drew away from him and exclaimed angrily, "I'll have you understand that I don't pursue men. They pursue me."

"But you attract them cleverly and knowingly, with your eyes, your lovely voice, and your beauty. You could do such a wonderful work for the Lord with that beauty and charm, if you'd only turn all of it over to Him."

"Perhaps I shall some day, when I've had my fun." She tossed her head as she rose and started back to the house.

He caught up with her and remarked, "Then it may be too

late, my dear. I'm more concerned about your soul than I am with anything else just now."

She gave him a surprised glance, but the thing she hoped for was not in his eyes, so she replied coldly, "Don't be so concerned, because I am not, not in the least."

Angela was sitting on the grass with William Mumford. He had been gloomy and disgruntled when Diana had left them and gone away with Keith and he had sought Angela without any excuse for his former neglect. Indeed, he seemed utterly oblivious of the fact that he had ignored her so completely.

"Don't look so glum," Angela advised as he sat down beside her. "You're no worse off than the others. Can't you see what she is doing to you, William?"

"No, I can't," he replied disconsolately. "At least I don't want to. I do see, but I love her so I keep hoping that perhaps my love will one day win out and she will love me."

"I wish it would happen if it will make you happy, but I'm afraid you're hoping against hope. She's older than you are, William, and Diana doesn't love anyone but herself just now. Perhaps she never will."

"She's liable to fall in love with that Yankee," he grumbled. "He's got everything that I don't have, looks and money and he lives out here where he can see her every day."

She smiled. "Don't be afraid of him. She's just interested in him because he's new. He's not falling for the bait as easily as she thought he would. I think he understands her better than anyone outside of her family. Don't be afraid of him. Cheer up and try to have fun today. Isn't that what you came for?"

"No. I came to be near Diana, even though she scarcely ever gives me a glance when the others are around. I was hoping that none of them would be here."

"Then you don't know Diana very well," she told him.

Presently he saw them coming across the lawn. Keith left her while she came toward them. Without a word of apology for leaving her so abruptly, William arose and hurried to Diana. She greeted him with a smile and Angela could tell by the look in his eyes that he was overjoyed. In a moment, however, she was greeting the others who had sauntered up and crowded William into the background. Angela sighed with sympathy for the boy so desperately in love and so unhappy because of it. Where would it end, she wondered. How well that she did not know what the tragic end would be.

9

THE GUESTS LEFT BEFORE DARK and the family retired earlier than usual, for they were tired after the long day, though Roger and Alicia had enjoyed the day thoroughly. Diana went to her room with very little to say, after a light lunch which they had in the breakfast room.

"Now that Keith has had the experience of a barbecue, how do you think he liked it?" Roger asked while they were eating.

"He seemed to be enjoying it," Angela volunteered. "I know that we enjoyed having him with us a part of the time, Dot and the rest of us very young people," she added with a grin at her father. "He was the only man who even looked at us most of the time. He's a dear. He said the sight of all that food made him drool and he surely did his share to make it disappear."

"What kind of a time did you have, Diana?" her father asked. "You seemed to be the center of attention, as usual. I hope the other girls didn't feel neglected. You didn't seem to be acting as a very good hostess to them."

"Angela was the perfect hostess, so why should I interfere?" Diana retorted. "Nothing I ever do seems to be right. I tried to make everyone have a good time."

"There was no need for that remark, Diana," her mother rebuked her. "You can do the right thing when you try. The trouble is that you so seldom try if it doesn't please you."

Diana did not answer, but finished the meal in silence

while Angela repeated some of the nonsense they talked about with Keith. She knew that Diana was displeased about something and she thought it must have something to do with Keith, for she had seen the expression upon Diana's face when she and Keith had parted after their little tete a tete under the trees. She smiled to herself. This fish wasn't proving easy to be hooked. He was the most difficult one she had ever encountered and Diana was not pleased about it. Well, it would be a good lesson for her if she never made any headway with Keith. He was too nice to be hurt by falling in love with Diana and she hoped he never would, for she liked him too much to see him hurt as William was being hurt.

The summer passed rapidly, for there was much to occupy the time. There were dinners and parties on the plantation and occasionally in town. Keith dropped in almost daily, either for a meal or for a visit in the evenings. And he and Diana went for frequent rides.

Diana had gotten over her huff at Keith's frank appraisal of her, but she had not given up her determination to make him fall in love with her. Since he had proved so difficult, it made him all the more interesting, for this commanded all of her skill and resources. She refused to be angry with him even when he spoke to her quite plainly about her soul and her indifference to the fact that she was a lost sinner. He used tact, but he tried in every way possible to make her aware of her spiritual condition. She listened and pretended to be interested, but he knew that her interest was only pretense and it grieved him, for the more he saw of her, the more potent her charm became until he feared that he was reaching dangerous ground.

He decided that perhaps he had better not see her so often and he visited the Wilborn's less often as the summer waned and autumn came. He had a good excuse to curtail his visits for there was much to be done about the house and the plantation. The cane which was sparse would not produce as large a sugar crop as it should have done and his income would be greatly reduced.

As the summer died, the war clouds with their winds of

destruction drew nearer, while the South watched the proceedings in Washington with growing anxiety. The daily paper carried headlines of debates in Congress, the angry accusations and hurtling blasts from senators who represented both sections of the country as well as the border states. Those in the South realized that the brunt of the war would descend upon them and they would face inevitable ruin which would follow if there should be war and if the North should win.

Men like Roger Wilborn prayed earnestly that war would be averted. They loved their nation and they dreaded the strife which would leave its trail of bitterness through generations to come. In their innermost souls they realized that the South must inevitably be defeated, even though they might be willing to shed their blood to keep that from happening.

Keith knew that if war should come, he would be ruined with the rest of the South. He would also be alienated from the closest and dearest friends he had ever had and he watched the situation with increasing concern. He was anxious to get the place in order as well as to get the cane cut before he would have to leave if war should come. He would not let himself dwell upon the thought of what would happen to him if he lived until the war should end if that dreadful possibility should become a reality.

November came and toward the middle of the month the slaves began to cut the cane and haul it to the sugar mill where it passed over the conveyers to the grinding machine at the end. The juice, a dirty, greenish liquid, fell into conveyers which took it to the huge open kettles where it began to bubble and boil.

The smell of boiling juice and the acrid fumes of molasses filled the air while the mill worked day and night so that the cane could be cut and ground before any possible danger of frost or early freeze. Planters had been known to lose their entire crop when taken unaware by early freezing weather.

Angela enjoyed this time of the season. She was on hand when the wagons brought in the cane and unloaded it upon the conveyers. She rode with her father as he followed the

Negroes where they worked cutting the cane and loading it on the big carts. Soon there would be *la cuite,* the thick syrup taken from the kettles just before the juice turned to sugar. Eaten with pecans, of which there were many dropping from the great trees which bordered the fields, it was a most tooth-some confection. Served upon hot pancakes it was delicious.

Keith had found the mill upon his place in such a state of neglect that he could not use it, so Roger generously offered to let him use his mill and Keith was thankful for the offer. This brought him to the plantation early and he remained late, as he followed the carts back and forth and he often remained for dinner when the day's work was finished.

Diana was more charming than she had ever been and vied with Angela in repartee. She seemed more beautiful than ever and he felt himself falling under her spell even though he knew her for what she was, shallow and vain and heartless. It did not worry him, however, for he knew that before long they would be moving back to the city and they would be sepa-rated, for he did not have a place in town. His grandfather had sold the family home there after his wife had died. He knew that the winter would be terribly lonesome, for the trips to town would be few and far between. The roads would be almost impassable when the winter rains set in and it would be a long unpleasant ride.

One evening in late November when the grinding was almost over and the Wilborns were making plans to pack up and close the house for the winter, he went over for a visit. There were other visitors there spending the night, a couple who were passing through on their way to town with two young people near Angela's age. He was on the point of leaving when he saw that they had other visitors, but they insisted that he should remain. It fell to Diana's lot to entertain him and she was more than willing to do this. The night was mild so she suggested that they go for a walk in the garden.

"We'll soon be leaving for town and this may be the last time I shall have to have a talk with you away from the others," she remarked as she made the suggestion.

"I shall miss you very much," he told her. "This summer has been one of the happiest I have ever spent. You people have been wonderful to me. You've made me feel almost like one of the family."

"We have enjoyed your friendship and we shall miss you," she replied. "I have enjoyed our rides. It was nice to have company and not have to ride alone."

He was silent and she continued, "I'm afraid I've been a big disappointment to you. I'm really sorry."

She did not say what was in her thoughts. He had been a big disappointment to her. He had been adamant to all her little devices to win from him some spark of romance. She had met with her first real defeat and it irked her.

"In a way you have," he admitted. "I was hoping you would change your outlook on life and realize that there is something else in life besides satisfying one's desire for pleasure in one's own way."

"I'm afraid it's hard to change a person's nature," she sighed. "I can't help it if I am the way I am. I was born that way, so how am I to blame for what I can't help?"

She was clinging to his arm for the way was dark under the trees.

"You can't change your nature, but God could if you would only yield that nature to Him. He would enable you to help others instead of hurting them. He could make you see that there is real joy in serving Him."

"Are you going to spend what may be our last time together for goodness knows how long, by preaching to me and telling me how bad I am?"

She spoke in pleading tones that brought a quickening of his heart even though he knew that she was only acting.

"Forgive me. I don't want to preach or to spoil this last hour together. I want to remember it always with pleasant thoughts, for we don't know what may happen before another summer rolls around."

"Are you really going to stay out here alone all winter?"

she asked. "I do hope you'll change your mind and come to town and stay with the Mayhews like they have begged you to."

"They won't let me pay board and I can't just go and live with them. That would be taking an unfair advantage of their friendship."

"I'm sure they wouldn't feel that way about it," she argued. "They have a big house and plenty of money and you would cause them no expense. And Dot would be delighted. She thinks you're a very wonderful person."

"Dear little Dot! I think she's a very wonderful little girl. She did her utmost to make me feel welcome when I went there as a stranger and they took me in because of their friendship for my father."

They were silent for a little while, then she said softly, so low that he could scarcely hear her, "I think you are a very wonderful person too."

He looked down at her and smiled in the darkness.

"Do you really?" he asked.

"I really and truly do."

Her voice was throbbing with tenderness while she leaned against him and laid her head upon his shoulder. She held up her face and her lips invited him.

He took her in his arms and held her close while he kissed her swiftly and fiercely, then released her.

"Why — why — did you do that?" she gasped, surprised, not at the kiss, but at the swiftness with which he released her.

"That was what you wanted, wasn't it?"

"How dare you say a thing like that!" she cried, angry at his cool calm voice.

"You invited me to kiss you, so I would have been very ungallant if I had refused. Why be angry because I did what you wanted me to?"

"Now you're being insulting!" she cried angrily.

She raised her hand to strike him but he caught it and held it tightly.

"Let me go!" she cried. "You talk as if I were a cast off creature of some kind, some sinful woman."

"That's just what you are, my dear, in God's sight. You are a sinful woman, though a very lovely girl. In His sight you are no different from a cast off creature."

"If I were a man, you wouldn't dare talk to me like that!" she blazed. "Your every word is an insult."

"I'm not being insulting, I'm just telling you the truth. In God's sight sin is sin and, since you are not saved, you are a lost soul and all lost souls look alike to God. If you were a man I wouldn't have had to say this. You've done everything in your power to make me yield to your charm and, now that I have yielded, you are furious."

"You call yourself a Christian and you think you are so holy while you think that I'm such a sinner. Yet you don't act any different from any other man who has had the opportunity to do what you just did, even if I did invite you, as you accuse me of doing."

"I confess that I didn't act like a Christian and I apologize, but that doesn't excuse you for trying to lead me on."

He drew her closer while he still held her hand, even though she tried to pull away from him, then he put his arm around her and held her there.

"Don't be afraid. I shall not kiss you again," he assured her. "But I shall have the memory of those lips against mine all through the lonely months ahead. I could love you, Diana, if I would let myself. In spite of what I know you to be, shallow and vain and selfish and absolutely heartless."

She drew away and he let her go. She faced him still furious.

"If I'm all of those things, then pray don't let yourself fall in love with me," she flashed.

"I won't, I promise you," he replied with a low laugh. "Whenever I feel that power of your beauty drugging my senses, I remember what you are and then your power over me is gone. I could never allow myself to fall in love with you, for any man who loves you is bound to suffer. I don't want that kind of love. I want the kind of love that makes a man happy."

"Let's go back inside," she said and turned toward the house.

When they joined the others and Angela saw her face and those flashing dark eyes and when she looked at Keith and saw how he looked, she knew that something momentous had happened out there under the trees. She wondered what it was. She hoped with all her heart, a hope that was half a prayer, that Keith had not yielded to Diana's wiles. She knew that Diana hurt those who loved her most. How she hoped that Keith would not be hurt! If she could have looked into the future, she would perhaps have prayed a little more earnestly that neither of them would be hurt, but she was thinking only of Keith, for she loved him very dearly as a friend and a Christian.

10

THE COOL TANG OF AUTUMN was in the air. The leaves were falling fast from the trees which would not keep their foliage through the winter, while the summer annuals were withered and dying. The big house looked deserted although the family was still there. The shutters were closed at most of the windows while inside, the draperies had been taken down and stored until the family returned in the spring.

Alicia stood this morning looking about her in the denuded room and there was a look of sadness in her dark eyes.

"I wonder if we will ever return here again," she remarked to Roger who came in and slipped an arm around her, putting his cheek against hers.

They were a handsome couple and age had not yet left its mark upon them. They were in the prime of life, a life that had been lived in happiness and companionship through the years of their marriage. Roger, taller than the average, had the same brown hair that Angela had inherited, though the girl's features were like her mother's. His was a strong face, though there was no sternness featured there.

"What brought on that gloomy thought?" he asked solicitously. "You don't feel ill, do you?"

"I never felt better," she replied as she rested in the circle of his arms, "but there is so much strife and such impending trouble in the very air that I fear for what the future holds. I'm afraid that before another summer there will be war and that may mean the end of our life as we know it now. How I do pray that God will undertake and keep us from war."

"Civil war will be a terrible thing," he replied. "It will tear families apart and break so many hearts. Brother will be fighting against brother and how terrible that will be! I fear that if Lincoln is elected, there will be trouble even before war should be declared. Already there is talk of secession in town. These hot-headed Creoles are not going to submit to the demands of the North to get rid of their slaves. They like the luxury of it all too well. I heard some talk that Louisiana may secede and be an independent state, war or no war."

"That would be terrible!" Alicia cried, turning and looking into his face with troubled eyes. "We couldn't exist as a separate republic. Don't those hot heads realize that?"

He smiled rather ruefully.

"Perhaps I shouldn't blame it all on the Creoles. Others feel the same way they do, though it was the suggestion of one of them. I can't blame them too much. We still believe in State's Rights and if those rights are invaded, we shall either have to secede or fight. We may have to do both."

"That's why I was wondering if we shall be able to come back here again next summer," she said sadly.

"Let us hope and pray that we shall," he replied as they went into the dining room which was also denuded of draperies and cut glass and silver.

"I hate to think of leaving here," Angela said as the girls came in to breakfast. "I've never had such a good time as I've had this summer. By the time I come back next summer, Little

Fellow will be a grown horse and he will have forgotten all the tricks I taught him."

"All!" Diana echoed. "I thought you said you could only teach him to come when you called him if you had an apple for him. If he didn't see the apple, he wouldn't come."

Angela giggled. "I guess you're right, Sis. At any rate, he won't even know me next year."

"If that's all you regret, you don't have much to worry about."

"I hate to leave Keith," Angela replied with a sidelong glance at her sister. "I've enjoyed having him for a neighbor, even though I didn't have the pleasure of riding with him."

"It was your own fault," Diana informed her coldly.

"I wonder." Angela smiled and changed the subject.

After breakfast she went into the kitchen as usual to have a little chat with Mammy Sue. She hadn't been with her as much this summer as she had in the past and the old slave realized that her "baby chile" was growing up and it wouldn't be long before she would lose those precious moments together with her.

"I'm glad that you're going back to the city with us," Angela remarked when they were seated in their usual place on the porch. "I was afraid Father would want you to stay here and sort of look after the others."

"I'se glad too, chile," Mammy replied. "I think I'se about got Nora and Gertie to where dey can do widout me, at least until de white folks gits back next year. Dat boy Jim has growed to be a fine overseer. He kin take keer of eve'thing in between de times when yo' pa comes out heah to look dem oveh. Marse Roger don' go off and leave his colo'd folks to get along de bes' way dey kin when he goes back to town. He sure takes keer of 'em."

"That's because he's a Christian, Mammy." Angela sighed. "The only disappointment of the summer is that Diana still won't give her life to the Lord. It looks like she's farther away from God than she ever was. I was hoping that Keith would change her, but he didn't succeed."

"I think she laks dat man a lot," Mammy observed.

"I don't know. I think she just wants him to like her a lot. I don't think Diana really cares for anyone but herself and I hate to think that. She could do so much for the Lord if she would only yield her life to Him."

"I see dat young Marse Ralph hangin' 'round you a lot dis summer," Mammy remarked with a sly look at Angela. "You done took him away f'm yo' sister?"

"I didn't take him away, Mammy. He took himself away. I don't know what happened, but Diana did something to him way back there in the spring before we came out here that made him very bitter toward her. He wouldn't tell me what it was, but he surely is through with her. He didn't even want to come to my birthday party, he said, because he would be where she was and he didn't want to even be polite to her. I did my best to make him have a good time and — so — we became friends."

"H'm! I'd say you wus a lot more'n friends, f'm de way he looks at you," Mammy replied.

"That proves that you've been spying!" Angela said, shaking a finger at her while the color mounted in her face.

It was true that she and Ralph Hastings had become more than friends during the latter part of the summer. Ralph had been smarting under Diana's rudeness when she had slapped him after leading him on to kiss her and he had sworn off of all girls, telling himself that he hated them all. When, however, he had been invited to Angela's party and had finally decided to accept the invitation, he found that she was entirely different from her sister. She was so genuinely friendly, with none of the coquette's wiles, that he forgot his boyish oath and they became friends. Before the summer was over they had become more than friends. Though Ralph had never so much as kissed her hand, she knew that he cared for her and she knew by the fast beating of her heart when he was near and the constancy with which he was in her thoughts, that she cared for him. With the resiliency of youth, she had overcome her girlish affection for William Mumford when he had ignored her so completely whenever Diana was around. She looked forward to being in town so that she and Ralph could see more of each other, even though she hated leaving the plantation and the life there which she enjoyed so much.

"I know what Diana will be doing just as soon as we get to town," Angela told Mammy. "She'll be slipping away to parties where there is dancing and she will be going to the opera at the new French Opera House, even though Father has told us that he did not want us to go. I heard her making plans for that with one of the boys just the other night when they were here."

"It sure will take a lot o' dealin' f'm de Lawd befo' He bring her to her knees. I hates to see her suffer, but if she do, it will be her own fault. She kain't blame it on no one else."

The night before they left Roger invited Keith over to dinner.

"I hate to think that this is our last meal together for so long," Roger remarked as they took their places at the table.

"We shall miss you, even though we hope to see you in the city occasionally, for we don't know what may happen before we dine here again."

"That is true. We don't know what the future holds for any of us," Keith replied. "However, it may not be too long before I see you again, for I've changed my mind about staying in town for the winter. The Mayhews have persuaded me to stay with them. When Mr. Mayhew came out here yesterday, he made me feel that I would be hurting their feelings if I didn't accept their offer. He showed me how I could still carry on here and yet live in town, just as you do. There will be so little to do on the place and I have gotten a good overseer at last, so there is no excuse for me to stay out here alone."

"Oh good!" Angela cried. "Now it will be just perfect when we go to town."

"Thanks for those kind words," Keith answered smiling with the others at her enthusiasm.

"It will be nice having you for our neighbor through the winter," Diana said politely, but without enthusiasm.

She could not forget that kiss. Her heart beat faster every time she thought of it, but her cheeks burned with indignation when she remembered Keith's frank appraisal of her. It bit deep into her pride, but she comforted herself with the thought that if he had not wanted to kiss her, he would never have done it, no matter how hard she might have tried to lead him on. And she didn't have to even half try to lead him on! That was quite a comforting thought. She'd make him care yet, no matter if he did say that he would not let himself fall in love with her. Men had said that before, but it hadn't worked. They fell in love before they knew it and in spite of all their brave talk and resolutions. He would be no exception.

Keith thanked her politely though his eyes did not linger on her face as they had so often done before. He turned and answered a remark from Alicia and appeared to forget her. He did not forget her however. The memory of her luscious lips against his had remained with him and, try as he would, he could not forget that kiss. He was ashamed of himself for having kissed her in the way he had, even though he told himself that she had it coming to her. But he could not be sorry that he had kissed her. He knew, as he had told her, that it was what she had wanted, but he also knew that it was what he had wanted almost from that first time they had met. He had been making brave resolutions to himself and had steeled his heart against her, but love heeds neither brave resolutions nor steely hearts. Love knew that hearts can be melted and good resolutions can be broken.

He did not remain long after dinner, for the Wilborns were to leave early the next morning and wanted to get to bed early. Diana did not offer to walk to the gate with him. She wanted to, but she was afraid of another humiliating experience and Keith was glad that she did not offer, for he did not want the temptation to be placed in his way again and he could not have refused her offer if she had made it. He told her good-by with the rest, knowing that it would not be for long.

Early the next morning they drove to town after Angela had made a last visit to the horse lot and had a brief session with her pony. The little dog Toby had been washed and combed and made ready for the time when he would be a polite and decent house dog again.

They arrived in town just as the city was beginning to stir for the day's activities. Carts were clattering over the cobble stones on their way to the French Market with their produce, while merchants were opening their shops and taking down the blinds from in front of their windows. It was cool and shady under the overhanging galleries of the stores along Canal Street, though the sun was already making its heat felt to those in the glare of its rays. It seemed much warmer in the city, for the summer still lingered even though the season was late for summer warmth.

When they arrived at the big white house on Esplanade, with its wide front porch and the tall columns and broad steps, the door was already open and the house maid was standing at the threshold to greet them while the yard boy came to take the horses to the rear and unload their baggage. The rest of their baggage would follow later on in a wagon from the plantation.

It was cool and inviting in the wide hall and Alicia remarked that it was good to be back home again in the city.

They went to their rooms and changed to other clothes, then gathered in the dining room where a lunch was waiting for them.

It was quiet and peaceful here in the large room with the bay windows and they could scarcely realize that out in the world beyond, the thunder of war was drawing nearer and that its storm would so soon envelope them all in a whirlwind of disaster and suffering.

11

ANGELA WAS AWAKENED THE NEXT MORNING by the loud clatter of the milk woman's cart as it rattled by. It stopped down the street and the woman rang her big brass dinner bell to announce her arrival at a customer's house. The milk was carried in a large two-wheeled cart in two big containers with a faucet. Housewives brought their pitchers out to have them filled. Roger had milk delivered from the plantation. He knew that it was not watered as it frequently was by the milk woman or man who delivered it.

Far in the distance Angela could hear the wailing cry of a free woman of color. *"Cala tout chaud!"* she called at intervals as she passed along the thickly populated section of the street where rows of double homes crowded against each other. The inmates of these double homes bought the small rice cakes which were still hot and thickly powdered with sugar. They were delicious and these colored women possessed a skill in making them that no one else seemed to equal.

Angela dressed hurriedly and slipped out of the house for a walk before breakfast. She loved the busy and interesting life of the city as much as she did the quietness of the plantation and she looked about her with eager eyes as she went down toward the river. She wondered, as she passed her home, if Dot Mayhew was up yet. Keith would soon be there and Dot would be in the seventh heaven of happiness, for she still had her girlish crush on Keith. She wished that Keith would fall in love with Dot, for Dot could make him happy, even if she was so much younger than he. It would be so unfortunate if he should fall in love with Diana, for then he would never be happy unless Diana changed and it would take a miracle for that to happen.

Angela strolled along past houses with green shutters still closed even though the morning was not cold, until she came to the mint, a large brick building behind a high iron fence. The faint acrid fumes of the acid used in the previous day's work still pervaded the atmosphere and made her cough. In the yard the stars and stripes were waving gently in the faint early morning breeze. It had already been raised upon the tall flag pole. Angela was proud of that beautiful flag and she felt like saluting it every time she saw it flying in the breeze, for she loved her country and was thankful that she had been born in a land where there was freedom of religion and where so many blessings abounded. She was sure that that flag was the most beautiful flag of any nation.

Down by the river she could hear the hum of the already busy market place, the old French Market which had existed for so many years. Through strife and distress the city had been occupied by French and Spanish rulers before it became a part of the growing America that had at last given the city and the whole territory of Louisiana its freedom.

A colored woman passed by with a tray of small cakes calling out in a loud singsong, *"Pain potates! Pain potates!"* They were small cakes made from sweet potatoes. Children ran after her buying the cakes and eating them on the spot. Evidently they had had no breakfast, Angela thought, as she saw them gobbling the cakes ravenously.

She crossed the street to wander through the market which was always an interesting place to her. She saw the little old wrinkled praline woman already seated by one of the pillars fanning the flies off of her pralines arranged in neat little stacks in a wide wicker basket. Angela was sorry that she had not brought her purse along, for she loved the delicious candy made from brown sugar and filled with pecans, also the pralines cooked with white sugar and thick with coconut.

"Pralines, Ma'mselle?" the old Negro asked hopefully as Angela stopped and smiled at her.

"I'm sorry, but I have no money this morning," Angela told her. "But I'll be back later to buy some. You haven't forgotten me, have you?"

"Non, Ma'mselle," and the old Negro shook her head vigorously while her wrinkled face broke into a smile. "I could not forget one so beautiful and so good to buy my pralines. I'm glad you come back home again."

"You're right, Mammy," a voice behind Angela said. "How could anyone forget a person so beautiful? Give her a couple of each kind and I'll take a couple myself."

"Where on earth did you come from?" Angela asked as she turned and saw Ralph.

"From following a beautiful lady," he replied. "I saw

you way in the distance and I thought I'd spy upon you and see where you were going. It's good to have you back again." His eyes told her what his lips had not yet uttered.

"I'm rather glad to be back," she admitted. "Though I did hate to leave the plantation. This was the happiest summer I ever had there."

"The happiest part of my summer was getting to know you," he said while the ardent look that accompanied the words brought a quick flutter to her heart and warm color to her cheeks.

"Thanks for those kind words and thanks for the pralines," she replied with a smile as he handed her the little bag containing the pralines. "I think I'd better be hurrying home or I'll be late for breakfast."

They crossed the street and walked back toward her home while they munched on the pralines. She had forgotten that she had said she should hurry.

"The nicest thing about knowing you, Ralph, is finding out that you are a Christian. You're the only boy I know besides Keith — and he isn't really a boy any longer — who is a Christian."

"Perhaps that's what made me change my mind about girls when I got to know you better," he told her. "I thought they were all alike, just — " he checked himself, realizing that he had made a blunder.

"You mean like Diana," she supplied for him. "I understand. Just what did she do to you to make you so bitter?"

"I'd rather not talk about it," he told her. "But she made me hate all girls for a while. You changed everything in my whole life and I thank God every day that He let me get to know you."

Angela was silent. She was hoping that he would say what she felt was in his heart, yet she was not quite ready for that to happen. It was rather an unromantic time and place and she had had a young girl's dreams of a garden in the shadows under a full moon when there was no one else to see or hear when the great event took place. There she would open her heart to the love which he would declare and to which she would be so eager to respond.

"When may I see you?" he asked when they had reached her home.

"Real soon," she promised. "It was nice seeing you this morning." She gave him a radiant smile as she added, "It started the day just right."

"What do you think it did for me?" he asked.

She did not answer but gave him a parting smile as she left him. As she went into the house she was still wondering what Diana had done to make him so bitter. When he had come to her party in the summer he would not even go near Diana, but she was glad to observe that before the summer was over, he had become more friendly toward her. Diana had been especially charming to him, hiding her intention to keep him dangling after her rebuff under the guise of the solicitous hostess.

She had apologized for her rudeness in one of their few moments alone and he had accepted it as graciously as he could and had assumed a more friendly attitude toward her after that. Diana was pleased with herself for having won this little victory. Ralph proved to be more than she had thought he was in the beginning. He was not just a young unsophisticated country boy. His family, which had recently moved to town, had wealth and standing in the community. For that reason she was sorry that she had rebuffed him so cruelly in the beginning of their acquaintance. She now felt that he would continue to be more friendly and would eventually be once more completely under her spell. What she did not know was that Ralph despised her, now that he knew her for the heartless flirt that she was. He had given her his first boyish love, but since that night when she had slapped him he had grown older rapidly and nothing she could do would ever make him change his opinion of her. Of course Diana did not know that he had fallen in love with Angela and that she now occupied all of his thoughts as well as his heart.

Angela met Diana coming down to breakfast.

"I was afraid I was late," she said as she joined her sister and went into the dining room with her. "I went out for a walk to see if anything had changed while we were away. It was a perfect morning for a walk."

"Was it?" Diana asked indifferently.

She was wondering when Keith would come to town and how soon she would see him again. She had not realized how completely he had entered her life even though she had been so angry with him for his cool aloofness and his keen appraisal of her. She wanted more than anything to change his opinion of her, yet she was not willing to do the one thing which would do that and that was for her to accept Christ as her Saviour. She was not willing to do that for she knew that she could not play the flirt's game of love if she yielded her life to the Lord. A Christian did not spend her time in winning men's love and then breaking their hearts.

"I met Ralph while I was down by the French Market," Angela told her.

"You did?" Diana was interested at once. "We must have him over one night real soon. Ralph is a dear and he is very good looking."

Angela glanced at her sister with a lift of her brows, though she did not reply. What was Diana up to now? If she set her trap for Ralph, she herself would never have a chance. Their romance would be nipped in the bud. She tried to stifle the anger that rose within her at the thought. Diana was not willing for any boy to escape her. She could do nothing but hope that Ralph would not fall into Diana's clutches.

In a few days the household was running smoothly in its usual winter routine and the young people and their elders began to gather there as they frequently did through the winter. The house was large enough, with its big double parlors and the large dining room, for a number of guests to enjoy delicious meals and a social time afterwards. As usual the younger set gathered in one room while their elders sat in another.

Diana was in her element. She was the gay and charming siren as well as the gracious hostess. Keith, who had come to town soon after their arrival, was a frequent visitor with the

Mayhews. He watched with serious eyes as Diana wove the spell of her beauty about the boys who always hovered near her. There was a worried light in his eyes. He was wondering what he should do in the days ahead of them through the winter. He felt that he should stay away from her, for to be near her as often as he had been during the summer was dangerous to his peace of mind, yet he thought it would be foolish to deny himself the pleasure of the association with the rest of the family because of her. He prided himself upon the strength of his will. Since he knew her so well and could see the cold calculating heartlessness that lay beneath that beautiful face with those lustrous black eyes, there should be no danger for him where she was concerned.

Diana, on her part, was more eager to please him and to have him think well of her than she was about any of the others. He kept their relationship on the basis of friendship and refused to change his attitude in spite of all her attempts to break through that polite, indifferent barrier.

In anger at her sense of defeat, she finally decided to give up and to let him alone. There were others, she told herself, others just as handsome as he who were already at her feet. There was Ralph upon whom she could try her skill. She would devote her attention to him and forget Keith. But she couldn't forget him and as the winter came on she became more and more irritated at her failure, the first she had ever experienced.

As the Christmas season approached, the gay life of the city reached its highest peak. There were parties and gay nights at the opera. The French Opera which was patterned after the European opera houses, was crowded at each performance with a gaily dressed audience.

Diana begged to be allowed to go, but Roger was firm in his refusal.

"No Christian should attend such a place," he told her.

"But I'm not a Christian!" she blazed. "And if being one means that I have to give up everything in life that is fun, I don't ever want to be one."

"You don't even know the meaning of fun," her father

said seriously. "I'll never give up trying to make you want to be a Christian and I'll never stop praying that you will, until the breath leaves my body."

One night there was a benefit concert with home talent furnishing the greater part of the program, while a professional singer was to be the featured attraction.

Since the entertainment was to be put on by home talent and was for a worthy local charitable institution, Roger decided that they would all go. The girls were both excited at the opportunity, for Angela had been anxious to see the inside of the opera house, for it was one of the newer buildings. Diana was hoping that Keith would ask her to go with him, but he went in the carriage with Dot and the Mayhews. They had arranged to have seats together in one of the loges. Angela was going with Ralph and young William Mumford was going with Diana. Diana did not quite know how this had happened and she was angry to have to be with William, for she would have preferred Ralph if she could not have been with Keith. But her father had bought the tickets and had asked the young men to go with them, so she could do nothing but be as gracious as she could.

The local talent gave a very enjoyable performance, but everyone waited with growing eagerness for the featured singer to make her appearance. It had been advertised that she would introduce a new song and they were eager and curious to hear it.

She finally made her appearance, the last on the program. She was a lovely young girl with a lyric soprano voice that was clear and melodious. She sang several numbers and then came the surprise number. Taking her place in front of the glaring spotlight, she began to sing in ringing tones of fire and melody,

> "I wish I was in de land o' cotton,
> Ole times dar am not forgotten.
> Look away, look away, look away, Dixie Land."

The audience sat silent and listened with rapt attention during the first verse and chorus, but as she reached the climax, they began to shout and clap and howl. She was recalled time and time again to repeat the song until she could scarcely sing a note.

Before long the new song was on the lips of everyone who had heard it that night and soon people on the street were singing the melody which was destined to be the battle song of a section of a nation at war and which has never failed to stir to enthusiasm and quicker heartbeat every Southerner down through the generations.

Keith went home that night with a burden upon his heart. His heart answered to the call of that lilting, simple melody, for his love was embedded in this southland where he had been born and with the people who were so near and dear to him and he felt the justice of their viewpoint about the disputed question of slavery. But his loyalty was bound up with his oath of allegiance which he had taken when he entered West Point and again when he had received his commission as lieutenant in the army of the United States. He had sworn to defend that flag with his life, if necessary, and he could not do otherwise than to feel bound by that oath.

He would be true to that oath, even at the cost of his life, for he believed with Abraham Lincoln, that the Union should be preserved at all costs. United as states in one common bond, they would grow to be the greatest nation on earth. Divided, they would perish, for they would become the prey of every foreign power. But that would mean the loss of all that had made his life so happy during these months, his plantation, his home, his friends — and Diana.

Why had he added her, he wondered. He smiled rather bitterly. He could not say. He would not say.

12

As CHRISTMAS DREW NEARER Diana and Angela were busy with shopping and wrapping gifts for their parents and friends and also the servants. The big tree was set in place in the front parlor on a large white cloth and it was decorated lavishly with strings of popcorn and strips of bright paper glued to form chains. Small candles, the hazard of every Christmas party were clamped upon the tree in colored candle holders.

The family usually exchanged their gifts immediately after breakfast when the servants gathered in the parlor just behind them, waiting with eager anticipation to receive their generous gifts. Roger usually gave them money while Alicia and the girls gave them clothing and trinkets which they could not buy. In the evening there was always a dinner party, after which the young people had a gay social time together.

Invitations were already out, having been delivered by one of the slave boys and everyone was looking forward to the usual delightful time at this season.

On the twentieth of the month came the appalling news that South Carolina had seceded from the Union. Newsboys ran through the streets carrying extras and shouting the disturbing news. Their papers were soon sold out while an anxious people read the glaring headlines and wondered what the result would be. There had long been the talk of secession, but deep in the hearts of most of the Southerners was the hope that it would never become a reality.

Roger read the news with an aching heart. He knew what it would mean. A nation which had struggled through pioneer days over the blood of those who had cleared the way through a wilderness of hostile savages and who had later on shed their blood on one battle field after another, a nation which had won independence and freedom for itself through years of struggle and suffering and which was fast rising to first place among the nations of the world would be rent asunder and set back in its march of progress. There would be wounds which might never heal and bitterness which would mar the relationship which must exist if the nation was to be preserved.

He felt that the other Southern states would eventually follow suit, for the fires of rebellion against the invasion of states' rights was already flaming in Pensacola and it only needed the firing of one shot to set the flames of war to roaring. And war would bring untold suffering as well as death.

The news cast a pall of gloom over the city for a little while, but with the irrepressibly gay spirits which were at their height at this season, the city recovered in a measure from its gloom and continued with the festivities they had planned.

Roger gave no hint of his feelings to his family, for he wanted them to enjoy this Christmas in every way possible. He had a foreboding that this would be the last of these festivities for a long time to come. Perhaps he would never live to see one such again.

The guests gathered as usual on Christmas night at the dinner and conversation flowed as it usually did, but there was a subdued atmosphere that hovered over the gathering, something almost tangible that took away the sparkle and usual gaiety even among the younger set. The girls were beginning to realize something that they had not allowed themselves to think about, that if war should come, and now it seemed inevitable, the most eligible young men would be swallowed up by the army and might never return. It was a horrible thought and it quenched even their gay spirits somewhat.

Keith was present, sitting opposite Diana at the table, and she glanced at him as often as she could, surreptitiously, wondering what his part would be if there should be war. She remembered what he had said when they first met him and she wondered if he still felt the same obligation to his oath of allegiance to the army of the United States. Would he remain loyal to his friends or to their enemies?

For the first time she felt pain in her heart at the thought of losing him forever. She had declared to herself over and over that he was nothing to her and that she almost hated him because he knew her for what she was, but she knew now that she had only been deceiving herself. She did not hate him. She would rather have his good opinion of her than that of anyone else. She felt that he spoke the truth when he had declared that he would never let himself fall in love with her. She had had evidence of the strength of his character when he had so deftly avoided her and had remained only politely friendly.

Keith was silent during the conversation which drifted inevitably to the political situation. He could not join in and speak truthfully without the risk of making enemies of his friends and he did not want that. He had hoped so desperately that war would not come and that he would not have to make a decision which would make such a change in his life. Finally, however, someone turned to him with a question.

"What do you think of the situation?" the man asked.

"I think it is most serious and I pray that some way, somehow, war may be averted," he replied. "I feel that war can never really solve any dispute."

"What do you think of the question of slavery and states' rights?" persisted the other. He knew that Keith had come from the North and there was a hint of hostility in his voice.

"I believe as you do, Mr. Heath, but I believe that the question could be settled by other means than war. I believe that Lincoln would desire peace above all things and that when he is inaugurated he will prove that, if he is given a chance. But I'm afraid that he will not be given that chance."

"What about slavery?" Heath persisted.

"I believe that even this question could be settled without war. All slavery is terrible, but I believe that if the South were given a fair chance to get rid of the slaves and to get adjusted to a new form of life gradually, there would be no need for war."

"Enough of such talk!" Mr. Mayhew intervened, determined to save Keith from any more embarrassing questions. "This is Christmas, so let's talk of peace and good will and let war talk rest until another more appropriate time."

They began to talk of other things, but the gaiety had vanished and the guests left much sooner than usual, leaving the family to put out the lights and retire while they felt the weight of the pall of danger which hung over them.

On the twenty sixth of January Louisiana seceded. It announced itself as an independent republic, as the political leaders had suggested some time previous. A state flag, depicting a mother pelican hovering over her young in the nest printed in gold on a blue background, was hoisted on the flag pole in front of the mint after the stars and stripes had been lowered and burned.

Many were there at the ceremony, among them Roger Wilborn and his friend Mayhew. There were tears in Roger's eyes as he saw the flag he loved and honored taken down and this new flag which seemed strangely out of place, rising in its place. Mr. Mayhew turned to him and his face was pale and his eyes were worried.

"I feel that this is the end of our life as we knew it," he remarked.

Roger nodded, too overcome by emotion to speak.

"If war comes, what will you do?" Mayhew asked.

"If they need me, I shall fight to the last drop of blood for my state but I shall do it with a broken heart."

They turned and walked slowly down the street.

Events moved rapidly in the days that followed. The governor ordered the state militia to seize every place belonging to the Union. The Union had only forty men on duty. These occupied the arsenal at Baton Rouge under Major Haskins. Five hundred state militia surrounded him. Bragg, who later became a general in the confederate army, persuaded Major Haskins that the Union was at an end and the major surrendered the arsenal with the honors of war. He left by boat for St. Louis, a heartbroken and beaten man. He was a one-armed veteran of the Mexican war and had known the dangers and the victory of war and he had been honored by his government for his gallantry in conflict. Now to be forced to surrender without firing a shot was a bitter dose, but he knew the futility of endangering the lives of his men with such a superior force against them.

Life was suddenly changed in the city. There were no more gay parties and the attendance at the French Opera dwindled until there was only a pitiful handful for the final performance of the troup which had been brought from the North for the season. They left and the opera house was closed, temporarily, the managers announced, but everyone felt that it would be for a long time.

The weeks passed and nothing drastic happened and people began to feel that perhaps there would be no war after all. Yielding to Diana's pleas, Roger consented to have an occasional small dinner party, but though the young people enjoyed themselves and seemed to forget the seriousness of the time, their elders were aware of it and the gaiety seemed to have been drained from them.

On Sunday the churches were crowded. In the presence of an impending danger, people who had had no thought of God before, suddenly became aware of their need of divine guidance and strength and though they were utterly ignorant of the only way to receive that strength, they went blindly to the house of God, hoping by some mysterious process to receive in their own way the comfort and freedom from fear that they sought.

Mammy Sue spoke of this one morning to Angela when they met for a little talk. They had not been together for some time and Mammy felt keenly the loss of these precious times with her beloved "chile." She went to church where the family attended, one of the large churches on Canal Street and sat in the section reserved for family servants or other colored people who cared to attend. The increasing attendance almost crowded them out.

"It shore is funny how folks run to de Lawd when dey is in trouble, and how dey fo'gits Him when dey ain't afraid any mo'," she remarked.

"It sure is, Mammy," Angela agreed. "If people would only seek the Lord when there is no danger, they wouldn't get so panicky when danger threatens them. Wouldn't it be wonderful if the people in control of the affairs of our nation were real Christians? Then we wouldn't have any war."

"Dat ain't neve' gonna be, ontil de Lawd come back heah and take oveh dis ole sinful world and rule ovah it. But befo' dat day come, we is all gonna be gone to meet Him in de clouds and den you'll see whut'll happen. All dese heah people who ain't nevah took time to think about de Lawd is gonna run to de churches and fall on dere knees and ask de Lawd to save 'em f'm all de misery what is comin' on dem. Den you'll see how dey wishes dey had a took de Lawd and served Him when dey had de chance to do it."

Angela giggled. "I won't be seeing it, Mammy, because I'll be just where you'll be, with the Lord. But I wonder where Diana will be."

Mammy uttered a sigh, deep and mournful.

"She'll be wid de rest of de sinners, if she don't mend her ways."

Tears came to Angela's eyes as she was forced to realize that this was true. She must pray more than ever that Diana would accept the Lord before it was too late.

13

THE COLD DREARY DAYS OF January drew to a close and February, which was usually the worst of the winter months, came in with rain and dark cloudy days, with bitter winds to make the season more unpleasant. The heavy clouds that blotted out the sun were no more dark than the clouds of uneasiness and fear which settled upon the hearts of the citizens of New Orleans.

Angela found much to occupy her time while she was being kept indoors, but Diana roamed around the house as discontented as a disembodied spirit. She was not interested in reading and she did not like to sew and she found little diversion in her sister's company.

They played an occasional game of checkers, but Angela usually won and that left Diana more gloomy than ever. She did not even enjoy playing the piano as she had in the past. Occasionally she played a few numbers and once or twice she ended by playing the new song of Dixie which she had heard at the opera house. But she could not even get a thrill out of playing that. Angela came in once while she was playing it and joined in with her voice, singing the chorus with zest, but the song reminded Diana of impending war and the possible loss of all her admirers and, worst of all, of Keith, if he should decide to go.

March was ushered in with a storm that seemed to shake the foundations of the house. Trees were stripped of some of their branches and shrubs were laid low. There was some damage to the wharfs on the river front and a few shacks were blown down. This storm was but a faint foreshadowing of the greater storm which was approaching with swift and merciless intensity. On this day Abraham Lincoln was inaugurated with the waving of flags and the blare of bands marching past the man who held the destiny of a nation in his hands as far as human agency was concerned and who would at all costs try to preserve the nation which he loved; the man who, if he had lived, would have spared the unnecessary suffering which the South was forced to endure through his successor and the scheming politicians who used him for their own personal gain and the desire for power and revenge.

Three days later the provisional government of the Confederacy which had been established at Montgomery as Capitol, passed the act of enlisting one hundred thousand men for one year's service. Louisiana had given up the false hope of becoming an independent republic and had joined the Confederacy.

When the call came for enlistments, many of the young men from the city went at once and were sworn in. Some of them were sent away almost immediately to take brief training.

On a Sunday evening after church, Ralph walked home with Angela. He had sat with her during the service and she had felt the thrill of his hand touching hers as they shared the hymn book together. The walk home was rather long, but she had asked permission of her father to walk with Ralph instead of riding in the family carriage. Roger knew that soon she would be deprived of this time of social fellowship, so he consented for her to go with Ralph.

Angela was glad that Diana had not come to church this

evening, for if she had, perhaps she would have monopolized Ralph as she had done so successfully on previous occasions.

They walked for a time in silence, then Ralph broke the silence.

"I'm leaving shortly for camp," he announced, "and I just had to see you before I go. I never get a chance to talk to you alone any more," he added dolefully.

"I know. Diana is trying so hard to be friends to everyone."

She felt that this was not quite the whole truth, but she couldn't let him know what her sister's real motives were.

He did not reply, but he smiled wryly in the darkness. He knew only too well what Diana's reasons were and there was not the slightest motive of mere friendship in them.

"I hate to see you go," she said while he was trying to gain the courage to tell her what was in his heart. "I have enjoyed your friendship very much. We have had such good times this year. It was, I think, the happiest year of my life."

"I know it was the happiest year of mine and it wasn't friendship that made it happy."

His voice was eager but suddenly he stopped, hesitating to say more. He remembered his first disastrous experience with Diana.

Angela waited tremulously, eager and tense, for him to go on, but he did not, so they walked in silence until they reached her home. The night was cold but the glow in their hearts made them oblivious of the cold. When they reached the steps he took hold of her hand and held it gently.

"Angela, I've tried all the way here to tell you what I wanted to say, but I just couldn't get the words out. You must know that I love you. Don't you?"

Her voice was lilting with joy as she replied with a low laugh, "Of course I do, now that you have told me."

"But you have known it all along," he persisted. "I tried to tell you how much I loved you every time I looked at you. I was afraid to speak the words, for fear that you would do what Diana did."

He caught himself and stopped suddenly. He had not meant to say that. He regretted it but it was too late.

"What did she do?" Angela asked.

"Let's not talk about her," he begged. "I'm sorry I let that slip. I didn't mean to say it, but she made me afraid to tell you how much I love you."

"You were in love with her, weren't you?" she asked slowly.

"In a way, I suppose I was," he confessed. "But what I felt for her was nothing to compare with what I have in my heart for you. She was so very beautiful, but I found that she had no heart. It cut deep, but when I met you, I was thankful that I had found her out. I love you, Angela, and I always shall. You are so lovely and you have much more than mere beauty. I love you very, very much. Could you say you care a little?"

"I do care, very much, Ralph," she answered quietly.

He took her other hand and drew her closer.

"Would you let me kiss you?" he murmured eagerly, with his face very close to hers.

She smiled as she whispered, "I was hoping that you would."

He held her close while his lips met hers, tenderly, and clung there. Then, while he still held her he said, "I want more than anything in the world to ask you if you will marry me, but I can't do that while this horrible war is so near. If I come back when the war is over, I might have an arm or a leg shot off — or I might not come back at all. I wouldn't want to hold you to any promise, but if I do come back, I want to marry you if you still love me."

"I shall be waiting for you to ask me," she told him. "And it will not matter to me whether or not you have a limb missing. You will still be you and I shall love you. And if you don't come back — " her voice broke for a moment — "I shall know that you are with the Lord. I shall still be waiting until He calls me too."

"How wonderful that makes me feel!" he cried as he bent and kissed her again. "Somehow I feel that God will spare me to come back to you. I hope that He will not keep you waiting too long."

"I shall pray for you every day until you come home again," she whispered as he kissed her goodnight and left her.

She stood there for a little while alone in the darkness, going over again and again those little moments in his arms with his lips upon hers. How wonderful love was and how much more wonderful to know that they were both not only in love with each other, but that they both loved the Lord. They were in the circle of His love and if it was for their good, He would keep Ralph safe and bring him home again to her.

There was a smile upon her lips and she hummed a little song as she went inside and up to her room. Diana was already in bed and seemed to be asleep. The song left Angela's lips as she passed her sister's door and looked in on her for a moment. How sorry she felt for Diana! She could never know the joy that possessed her now, for Diana could never know such love as she possessed. For her there would be nothing but scheming to conquer and no feeling of happiness when she had conquered, for there was no real love in her heart for anyone but herself. So she had won Ralph's love in the beginning. And she had taken William away from her. How selfish she was! Would she ever be any different?

Angela held no bitterness in her heart against her sister, only thankfulness that Ralph had found her out and had been free to love herself. She was glad that Diana had taken William from her. He could never have made her as happy as Ralph would, for he was not a Christian.

When she knelt by her bed Angela poured out her heart to God in thanksgiving for the joy that had come to her. She prayed that if it was His will, that Ralph would be kept safe throughout whatever conflict the future might bring and that he would come back to her safe and very soon.

14

ANGELA DECIDED THAT SHE would not tell anyone about Ralph and herself. That would be her precious secret. If he should return from the war, it would be time enough to let the family know. She smiled to herself in the darkness. He had not asked her to marry him but she knew he would. This precious thought would be something to make the long bleak days when he was away a little less gloomy.

Ralph came over to tell the family good-by just before he left. Diana was effusive in her regrets over his leaving and in expressing her hope that he would not be gone very long. If one had seen her, not knowing the truth, they would have supposed that it was these two who were in love. Ralph looked bewildered and said little. He did not stay very long and did not have a chance to talk to Angela, but she threw him a swift, surreptitious kiss as he left and he gave her an understanding smile in return.

As Diana watched him go she was more sorry than ever that she had rebuffed him as she had in the beginning. He was a fine looking young fellow and he had much more in worldly goods than Keith would ever have. It would have been pleasant to know that he carried love for her with him into battle. She wondered if he cared still, or if he had not yet found it in his heart to forgive her completely. She was vain enough to believe that he still cared. When the war was over there would be fewer eligible young men on hand and she would not be happy unless she was surrounded by admirers. She was determined that he should be one of them.

Young men began to leave in increasing numbers and the social life of the city was at a standstill. A few gathered in the evenings to talk the situation over, but the gaiety had vanished. In some quarters there was unrest among the slaves and in many places where they had been mistreated, they were escaping and trying to reach some northern state where they could find refuge. Many of them were tracked down by bloodhounds and brought back to suffer greater cruelties because of their attempt to escape.

There was no sign of discontent among Roger Wilborn's slaves. He paid an occasional visit to the plantation to see how they were getting along and he found affairs there just as they had been while he was there. The slaves seemed happy and contented and the fields were being cleared for the spring planting.

Keith did not come over very often. He had been there only once after the call from the Confederacy had been issued and the family wondered why he did not come. Keith was fighting a battle with himself and he knew that he could not think clearly unless he was left alone and away from the lure of Diana's charm.

Spring came early toward the end of March and Alicia wondered if they would be able to return to the plantation. The garden was beginning to bloom again. Roses in great masses filled the air with their fragrance. They had been trimmed during the winter and their blooms were large and beautiful. Birds were busy building nests in the trees and making the air vibrant with their songs and brief quarrels, voiced in piercing cries of anger from the mocking birds and the blue jays.

When Angela saw the little pair of wrens fussing and warbling as they built their tiny nest in a nearby tall shrub, she knew that spring had really arrived.

The storm center swirled over Fort Sumpter at Charleston, the hotbed of secession. Anderson's forces were so far outnumbered and his position so hopeless that he had to decide between surrender or the annihilation of his men when the batteries across the bay began firing on the fort. General Beauregard, with the true chivalrous spirit which had been a tradition of the South, offered Anderson such honorable terms of surrender that he could not refuse. On Sunday, the fourteenth of April, Anderson, with his little garrison, stood at attention and saluted the stars and stripes, then to the strains of Yankee

Doodle, they marched on board the transport waiting to receive them.

The first shots had been fired which were to plunge a divided nation into a long and bitter war, when blood would be shed and lives would be blasted and a nation would stagger from the conflict with wounds which would take more than a generation to heal.

Lincoln issued a call for seventy-five thousand volunteers for three months. He thought, with others in high official circles, that the conflict would last just a short while. They knew little of the indomitable spirit of the South, nor its courage and willingness to fight to the death or to suffer any privation, in order to win what was a lost cause from the beginning. The South was fighting for the right to live their lives as they thought they had a right to live them, while the North was fighting to uphold a principle which they thought was just and which, at its foundation, was right. They failed to realize that there were two ways of upholding that principle and that they had chosen the wrong way — war.

New Orleans wakened on that Monday morning to the news that Fort Sumpter had been fired upon. Heavy hearts and forebodings turned to dreadful realization as war became no longer a dreaded possibility but an agonizing fact.

There was scarcely a word spoken that morning at breakfast in the Wilborn family. When Angela and Diana came in, they saw the headlines in the paper as Roger showed it to them. They took their places at the table and tears filled their eyes when he asked the blessing. He prayed as he had never prayed before that God would avenge the wrong and give victory to the right, no matter which side might be wrong or right. His voice trembled and broke before he finished and Alicia sobbed audibly. Angela prayed silently while tears fell from her eyes, but her prayer was for Ralph's safety. She was not thinking of the right or wrong of the war, but only of him.

That evening Keith came over. Roger met him at the door and greeted him gravely.

"Come in, my boy," he said. "It's good to see you again.

We have missed you. I'm sure your heart is as heavy as ours at the news, for we both know what this war will mean to everyone, but most of all to us of the South."

"That's why I haven't been here before," Keith told him as he followed Roger into the living room. "I've been waiting and trying to decide what I should do. Now that I've decided, I came to tell you good-by."

He greeted the rest of the family, but his eyes sought Diana as she watched him silently, her brooding gaze fixed upon him.

"Did you say you were going away?" Alicia asked as she greeted him.

"Yes. I received my recall several days ago, but I was waiting and hoping and trying to decide what I should do. I shall be leaving tomorrow for active duty with my command."

"You mean that you're going to fight against us!" Diana cried while her eyes flashed.

"I feel that I can do nothing less than answer the call of duty," he said gravely.

He knew what he was facing and it seemed the darkest hour of his life. He was separating himself from those he held most dear and from the girl who had entwined herself in his heart, but who now showed by her voice and her blazing eyes what she thought of him. He felt that she hated him.

"So! In return for our friendship you will be coming back to kill us!" She blazed.

"Diana! That is uncalled for. Be quiet!" her father commanded.

"Isn't it the truth?" she argued wrathfully.

"No, it isn't," Roger told her. "You put it too brutally, even if it was the truth. Keith has a right to his views in this matter just as we have ours. Give him the privilege of doing what he thinks is best."

"It isn't a matter of feeling, Mr. Wilborn," Keith said slowly and painfully. "It is a matter of duty and of principle. When I was admitted to West Point, I took the oath of allegiance to the flag of my country and when I received my commission I again took the oath to defend that flag with my life, if necessary. Now I'm called upon to keep my oath, no matter how great a sacrifice it may mean nor how much sorrow it may cause me. I would feel like a traitor if I failed to keep my oath."

"How will you feel if you should ever come back here to fight against us?" Diana asked in spite of her father's reprimand.

"I hope and pray that that may never happen," he replied earnestly. "I should feel like an even greater traitor, but I would have to obey my command. I would rather kill myself than to see any one of you come to any harm."

He included the family but his eyes were on Diana. He turned to Roger and spoke appealingly.

"You understand, don't you? My heart is here in the South and my feelings are the same as yours, but my adopted state, the one in which I grew up, has called me and the President to whom I owe my allegiance has called me and I cannot refuse to go. Can you forgive me for having made this decision? No one but God knows how hard it has been. This has been the greatest battle that I shall ever have to fight, I'm sure."

"Of course we forgive you, my boy," Roger said with tears in his eyes and a voice that trembled in spite of himself. "I pray that you will one day come back to us and that we can forget this horrible time if the Lord let's us live through it."

Keith rose to go, then turned to Diana.

"May I see you for just a little while before I go?" he asked.

She did not answer but the others told him good-by and left him alone with her. Angela whispered to him as she told him good-by that she would pray for him every day until he returned safely.

Keith turned to Diana when the others had left and said, "You don't want to talk to me, do you?"

"Why should I? What is there to say? You're joining the ranks of our enemies and I have nothing to say to an enemy."

"That is so very like you," he remarked and smiled sadly

at her. "There is something that I must tell you before I go, for I may never return."

She stared at him through somber eyes without replying.

"I don't know why I should want to tell you," he continued, "but I want you to know what I thought I would never say to you. I suppose I'm saying it because there is so little chance of our ever meeting again. I want you to know that I love you. Why, I do not know. I have asked myself that a thousand times, but it's true, even though I don't know why. I said I never would fall in love with you, but I was a poor ignorant fool to think that my will could win out against your beauty and your charm. Even though I know you are vain and shallow and utterly heartless, I love you. I love you with all the love of my lonely heart and I suppose I always shall, even though I know you despise me for what I have decided to do."

Her lip curled scornfully and her words came coldly and bitterly.

"I would never marry you, even if I loved you with all my heart. I would hate you even while I would be loving you, for fighting against my people."

He smiled, but the smile was mirthless as he said, "My dear, I have not asked you to marry me."

She caught her breath in shocked surprise at his words.

"I would never marry you, even though I love you so much," he told her as he regarded her. The smile had vanished.

"Then your words are an insult!" she cried.

She was ashamed that he had her at a disadvantage when she had jumped to the conclusion that he wanted to marry her.

"I'm sorry you feel that way," he replied. "The love of any honorable man is an honor when it is bestowed upon a woman, not an insult. I at least have honor, if nothing else."

"Love without marriage is no honor," she retorted. "Why did you tell me that you loved me if you had no thought of marriage?"

"I don't know why," he repeated. "I just wanted you to know that you have one more victim to add to your list. That may give you some satisfaction in the days to come when many of those victims may lie upon the battle field. I could never marry you and I would never want to. You would never make any man happy, for you would never be true to any one man unless your nature was changed by the power of God and I'm afraid that you will never give God a chance to change that nature. You are not a Christian, Diana, my dear. That is why I could never marry you, no matter how much I love you."

"I think you had better be going," she said as she rose. "You have already said too much."

"I shall pray that you will give God a chance," he said as he stood near and looked down into her lovely face. "Then, perhaps, when this war is over, if I should live, you would learn to love me and I would ask you to marry me."

"I wouldn't marry you if you were the last man on earth!" she cried furiously. "I never could love you. I despise you!"

He turned and went to the door. She followed him and they stood for a moment in the dim light of the hall.

"Would you grant me one last favor, even if you do despise me?" he asked.

"Why should I? What is it?" she asked.

"Once I kissed you without your permission, because I knew that was what you wanted. Now I ask you if you will let me kiss you before I go. May I, even though you do despise me?"

He waited, looking at her eagerly, hopefully, humbly.

"No! I will not!" she blazed. "Why should I? So that you may leave here laughing at me as you've always done?"

"There would be no laughter in my heart, Diana. There's only sadness there. But I would have one sweet moment to live over again in the dark days ahead and in the future about which I know so little. Could I laugh at something which would mean so much to me?"

She did not answer, but turned away and he opened the door and went outside, his heart heavy and his soul sick within him. Suddenly she turned and followed him outside into the darkness.

"I will let you kiss me," she conceded. "After all, we were once friends."

He took her in his arms and whispered, "And we shall one day be friends again, God willing."

He kissed while he held her close and he knew that her lips answered his.

As he released her with a final, "God bless you, my dear!" and went down the steps while the door closed behind him, there was a song in his heart in spite of the heaviness and sorrow there. He knew in that moment, that, in spite of her anger and her bitterness, that she did not despise him.

"God help her!" he murmured as he opened the gate and walked rapidly down the street. "May she one day give You a chance to deal with her soul and to make her what she could be if she would only let You."

15

DOT MAYHEW CAME OVER TO SEE Angela just after Keith had left. Her eyes were still red from crying. They went outside and sat in the swing on the wide back porch.

"It's so terrible, his going away to fight with the North," Dot remarked. "He is so wonderful and I liked him so much. I was almost ready to fall in love with him even though I knew he didn't even think of me in that way. And now he's gone to join our enemies. I couldn't ever think of him as an enemy, Angela. Could you?"

"No, I couldn't," Angela replied. "He only did what he thought was the right thing to do and, like Father said, he has a right to his opinion just as much as we do to ours. I'm just sorry that he couldn't have been on our side."

"In his heart I'm sure he was," Dot sighed deeply. "That's what he said. He kissed me good-by and called me little sister.

Mother and Father smiled, but there were tears in Mother's eyes and I couldn't keep from crying."

Diana came out just then and joined them. Usually she did not mingle with Angela's friends, for she felt so much older and their interests were not the same, but today she was so utterly miserable that she could not afford to be particular and she felt the need to talk to someone.

"I know you'll miss Keith a lot," Dot offered dolefully.

"We should be glad he's gone," Diana replied. "If his sympathies were with the North, then he should be there with them."

"Why, I thought you liked him," Dot exclaimed in surprise.

She did not notice the bleak look of desolation in Diana's expressive eyes, but Angela saw that look and she felt that Diana's words belied her real feelings. She suspected that her sister was grieving over Keith's going even more than Dot could imagine, but she knew that Diana would never betray her real feelings. She wondered what Diana and Keith had talked about in those last few moments alone. What they had said had been said very quickly, for Diana had come up to her room soon after they had left her and Keith together. Diana had shut the door between their rooms with a bang, which was a very evident indication that she wanted no communication from her. Diana often shut the door between them when she was angry with her or when she had been reprimanded for something which she did not want to discuss with her.

Angela suspected that Diana cared more for Keith than she would ever confess and she knew at last that what she had feared had come to pass, that Keith was in love with her. She had seen it coming and had regretted it for his sake. But now war had come between them and no one knew what the future would hold for either of them.

On the seventeenth of April, just three days after the fall of Fort Sumpter, Virginia seceded. Three days later, on the twentieth, Robert E. Lee resigned his commission in the army of the United States.

He had walked the floor all night, torn between two loves

and two loyalties, love for his country and the flag it flew and love for his native state and the Southland of which it was a part. When the night was over and day had dawned, he had fought his battle and had made his decision. He felt that his loyalty was, first of all, to his native state.

He wrote to General Winfield Scott, saying, "Save in the defense of my native state, I never desire again to draw my sword."

He was opposed to slavery and both his own slaves and those which belonged to his wife had long been free. None of them wanted to leave and they had remained upon his place, just as Roger's slaves had remained, working under the same conditions but free to leave at any time they desired.

He wanted emancipation to come from the slave states themselves as in time it would have, if they had been given the opportunity and due regard to compensation.

Lee's resignation from his command was a blow to those in authority, for they recognized in Robert E. Lee what the world has since recognized, the qualities that he possessed which made him not only one of the world's greatest soldiers, but which belonged to a Christian and a gentleman of the highest character.

General Scott made a statement which came from his heart, that Lee was worth more than fifty thousand veteran men. When Robert E. Lee finally surrendered his sword to General Grant at the war's end, he was still an undefeated leader who cared more for the lives and suffering of his worn and weary troops, than he did of the chance of winning more victories. It was in recognition of the greatness of this man that General Grant returned to him his sword and let him depart with all the honors of war.

Immediately after his resignation, Lee was put in command of all Virginia's forces. Lee knew full well what his resignation would mean to him financially. It meant the loss of everything, home and fortune and the comfort of life as he had always known it, but he counted these things but loss while he entered into a conflict which tore at his heart, yet to which he gave all the skill and ability that he possessed. He so skill-fully maneuvered the forces which were ultimately under his command, that the war was prolonged far beyond the expectations of a much harrowed and sorrowful man in the White House, who admired Lee's courage and genius, even while he was hoping for his defeat, a defeat which, under God was best, yet which might not have come if others under Lee had had his skill and if starving men had not been forced to fight to the death.

As the war progressed in its initial stages, the heart of the South beat high, for the men in gray were pushing their way to the north and their hopes for ultimate victory grew with the reports of each successful battle.

Gradually the tide began to turn and the Confederate forces were pushed back farther and farther into the south. The Confederate states farther to the north were feeling the pinch and privation of war, but as yet Louisiana had not felt the suffering which was to come later on.

Roger rode back and forth from the plantation, but he decided that they had better not move there for the summer, at least not until they were sure that the war would not come their way. They kept hoping that the South would either win or that a truce would be declared before the actual conflict should reach them. Louisiana was so far away from the center of the war that they kept hoping that they would escape. However, the Mississippi was one of the main sources of supply from abroad to the Confederate forces and it could not long escape the attention of the Union forces in their determination to cut off every avenue of help to the Confederacy.

Diana found life dull and she grew more unhappy and discontented as time passed. There were only a few of her boy friends still at home. Most of them were the very young ones, boys she had humored in their admiration when there were no more interesting ones at hand. Among this number was young William Mumford. Diana allowed him to come to see her occasionally, for there were so few others and she had known him so long and he had been so faithful that she was glad to have him come to break the monotony.

One afternoon when he came he was so gloomy and depressed that she wondered what had happened. Usually he was just the opposite, cheerful and full of fun.

"Johnny came home last night," he told her.

Johnny was one of her friends, though he had always been on the fringe of her circle, a timid, quiet young man who had been a teacher in one of the schools.

"He's lost a leg," William continued. "He got it the first day he was in battle. He looks terrible and is down in the depths for sure. They'll be needing more men soon and I hear they're going to start conscripting them. Then I'll have to go."

"I thought you wanted to go," she said, surprised at his words.

"I did want to go, just like I told you in the beginning, and I would have gone long ago, if it hadn't been for Mother," he said sadly. "I'm all she has and she needs me. She's getting worse every day, it seems. It would break my heart to have to leave her all alone."

Diana remembered about his mother. She had never been quite the same mentally after her husband had been drowned. His body had never been found. She was sorry about Johnny, but his tragedy made her think of Keith. Perhaps he was also in the thick of the conflict and the same thing or worse might happen to him.

She told the family about Johnny. He was the first casualty among their friends to return. They knew that others might be in hospitals behind the lines or in some prison, or, worse, they might be lying dead on some battle field. The horror and tragedy of war was brought home to them more forcibly and it depressed their spirits as they thought of what the future might bring. Angela was thinking of Ralph, though he had never been out of her thoughts for long. She had not heard from him and she was afraid that she might never be able to. It was almost impossible to get any news from those in the battle zones.

The Louisiana planters began to feel the effects of the war

as the time came for the harvesting of their crops. The markets which they had supplied were cut off and the sugar planters were not able to ship to foreign markets as they had usually done. Shipping was cut to the minimum, for vessels of the navy intercepted ships as they left the river and reached the gulf. They were either fortunate enough to turn back or they were captured as prizes of war. Poverty began to spread its pall of suffering over the state which had not yet felt the devastation of battle.

Only too soon, however, the surge of conflict rolled down upon the state which had already suffered under enemy invasions in the past.

Christmas came again, but there was no dinner party at the Wilborn's this year. There was no Christmas tree with the gay decorations and tiny candles. The family exchanged gifts, but they were simple and inexpensive. Prices were high and money was growing more scarce with each passing month. The Mayhews came over in the morning for a quiet visit, but they did not remain long. The memory of friends and loved ones who might be among the missing or who might be suffering the agonies of wounds took all the joy from them.

Dot asked Angela if they had heard from Keith, but of course they had not.

"How could you expect to hear anything from him?" Diana asked. "He is with our enemies now and he is one of them. Why should we want to hear from him? We should be glad that he is gone, now that we know what he is."

"Aren't you just a little bit hard on him?" Mrs. Mayhew asked. "He did what he thought he had to do. We know that his heart was here, but his loyalty was with his President and the flag under which he had served."

"That's not the way General Lee felt about it," Diana retorted. "He put his native state before his country. I think he was right and that Keith was wrong." Her voice was bitter.

"I thought you liked Keith," Mrs. Mayhew remarked, surprised.

"I did until he became an enemy," Diana answered.

"He could never become your enemy, my dear," Mrs. Mayhew said with a smile. "He liked you and your family too much for that ever to be possible."

Diana did not reply. Angela felt that her bitterness and her harsh words were only covering up a sentiment which was far from what she professed to feel for Keith, just as she had that afternoon with Dot.

On February the twentieth, David Glasgow Farragut arrived at Ship Island on the Hartford. Ship Island was a sandy stretch some twelve miles out from the Mississippi shore and served as a breakwater with one or two other small islands, between the Gulf of Mexico and what was known as the Mississippi Sound. There was a lighthouse on the island but no one else but the keeper lived there, for there was no vegetation and only a scant fringe of trees scattered over the island.

Farragut was planning to enter the Mississippi and thus cut off all communication between New Orleans and every foreign power. This would prevent them from receiving any help from any friendly nation.

Forts Jackson and St. Philip guarded the entrance to the river. Farragut planned to run past the forts. While he was waiting for his reinforcements to arrive at Ship Island, preparations were being made to prevent him from entering the river, for, beyond the forts, the city would be unprotected and at the mercy of the enemy. A boom, as the barricade was called, was strung across the river. Three schooners were chained together in the middle of the river and attached to each bank. Tension increased as the news reached the city and panic seized many hearts as they waited for what would follow.

Finally Farragut's reinforcements arrived and he sailed for the mouth of the river. He had four men of war, four other ships and nine new gungoats. They steamed through the narrow channel among the mud flats at the mouth and the sandbars beyond and up toward the forts. Though the forts thundered valiantly from their batteries and shells screamed at the enemy, Farragut's fleet succeeded in breaking through the barricade and steamed up the river toward the city, a hundred miles or so above them.

General Lovell evacuated his troops from the city. He knew that his soldiers could never hold out against such a superior force and he sought to save his men from capture. They could be of greater help to the Confederacy by fighting elsewhere than being confined in some Northern prison.

Left to themselves, without military defenders, the citizens went wild with anger and fear and the determination to make it as difficult as possible for the enemy when he arrived. On the levee, waiting to be shipped, were bales of cotton and barrels of sugar and kegs of molasses. There were meats of all kinds, salted and stored, waiting for transportation up the river. Along the wharf there were tug boats and small gunboats, as well as freighters.

The boats were set afire and floated blazing down the river while many of the citizens, gone wild, set the cotton and other goods on fire. They blazed in a smoky conflagration while molasses ran like rivers into the gutters along the streets near the river.

All night the city glowed in the lurid light of her own incendiarism. The next morning, from the old Christ Church belfry on Canal Street, the bell tapped the alarm. Those who had not been out the night before poured forth from their homes. A rabble held riot in the streets. Men, women, and children staggered under loads of pilferings from the conflagration. Everyone was shouting, "The Yankees are here! The Yankees are here! They have come!"

Burning boats, blazing cotton and a howling mob greeted Farragut's arrival.

There had been no sleep in Roger Wilborn's home that night. The girls were together in Diana's room where they could see the lurid glow of the flames and could smell the acrid odor of smoke and burning sugar and salt meat. They could hear the howling mob that ran through the streets as dawn came and despair filled their hearts. They lay down for a little while and tried to sleep when they were too tired to stand, but they could not stay in bed for long. Angela put her arm around Diana and she felt Diana shudder as a sob tore at her throat.

"This is the end," Diana sobbed. "It's the end of everything for us."

"It seems like the end of the world," Angela whispered as they watched the clouds of smoke with the flames bursting through and heard the cries of the mob.

The breakfast bell sounded and they went down just as they were, without even remembering to wash their faces which were streaked with tears.

Roger's face was solemn as he prayed before they ate. He prayed for protection for the city and that God would speedily bring an end to this terrible war and bring peace to the nation now torn apart. He knew that before peace came, they might be led through deep waters, but he also knew that he had God's promise. He read that passage from Isaiah forty three. "When thou passest through the waters, I will be with thee; and through the rivers they shall not overflow thee: when thou walkest through the fire thou shalt not be burned, neither shall the flame kindle upon thee."

None of them had any appetite and the meal was finished soon and in silence.

16

EVERY EFFORT TO SAVE THE CITY from Farragut had failed. The burning boats drifted downstream without hindering the enemy fleet and the way was open for the capture of the city.

On the twenty-eighth of the month the two forts at the river's mouth were forced to surrender and the Federals were in complete control of the situation. A landing party came from the fleet amid the jeers and cries of the angry mob, but when they saw howitzers being unloaded, their cries were silenced while they watched the proceedings with gloomy despair.

The troops marched up Esplanade from the river to the United States mint not far away. A barge crew entered the enclosure and lowered the Confederate flag which had waved there so triumphantly, and the stars and stripes of the union flag was hoisted in its place.

Anger and consternation swept over the crowds of silent people who saw the Confederate flag lowered, but they could do nothing but watch and seethe with wrath and the sense of defeat. Young Mumford was in that crowd of angry men. There were several other young fellows with him like himself, who had wanted to join the Confederate army, but for various reasons, had been unable to do so.

When the troops had left the mint, the boys went to the Wilborn home to tell what had happened. Diana saw them coming and hurried to open the door for them. She was eager to hear the news.

"Those Yankees took down our flag from the mint," William told her. "They've put guns down on the levee and at the head of Canal Street. They're taking over the city."

"Why did you let them tear our flag down?" Diana asked. "The city hasn't surrendered yet. They had no right to do that."

"How could we stop them?" one of the boys asked. "They would probably have shot us if we had tried to stop them. What do they care whether or not the city has surrendered? They're here and we have no soldiers to protect us."

"Are they still at the mint?" she asked.

"No," William told her. "They left as soon as they tore the flag down. One of the men threw it on the ground and put his foot on it. I felt like tearing him to pieces for doing that."

"Then why didn't you do the same thing with that Union flag?" she demanded.

"What do you mean?" William asked.

"I mean go tear that flag down just as they did ours.

Show them that we still have men, even if the soldiers have gone."

"Do you think we should do that?" William asked. "It might only bring trouble on us."

She gazed at him with contempt in her eyes.

"Are you afraid?" she sneered. "I'd tear it down myself if I were a man. There are no soldiers there now, so why don't you go down there and take that flag down? That is, if you're not afraid. Show these Yankees that we are not afraid of them and that we won't submit to insults to our flag, even if they do have guns and battle ships."

The boys stood there in silent indecision while her eyes swept over them and made them feel that she thought they were cowards for not doing what she had suggested. Finally William spoke.

"If that is what you want us to do, I'll do it," he declared. "If they kill me, they kill me," he added with a shrug.

"They won't kill you, so why be afraid?" Diana assured him. "Go and take it down now before the soldiers return. I wish that we had another Confederate flag to hang there in its place."

"Come on, fellows, let's go," William said.

He went down the stairs, followed by the others who hesitated a moment, then went reluctantly with him. Diana watched them go down the street and her eyes flashed with triumph. These Yankees would find that the people of New Orleans could not be intimidated so easily. Just then Roger came out.

"What's going on?" he asked.

"William and the boys were here," she told him. "They said that some men from the boats had torn down our flag from the mint. I sent them back to tear down the Union flag."

"Diana! Why did you do that?" he cried in angry amazement. "You may have sent those boys to their death. What did you hope to gain by urging them to do such a rash and foolish thing?"

"I want our enemies to know that we still have some fight left in us, even if we are at their mercy," she retorted.

"And what if they do not show mercy? What if William

and the others are sent away to some northern prison? How will you feel to know that you have been responsible for that?"

She shrugged. "They won't. There are no soldiers there now and I'm sure that none of our people who might see them will ever tell who did it."

"I hope that you are right." He shook his head sadly as he went back into the house.

Sailors and soldiers marched with fixed bayonets up Canal Street and turned at St. Charles, continuing on to the City Hall. A loaded cannon was placed in front of the entrance to the building and the Mayor was ordered to surrender. He came down the steps slowly and stood in front of the cannon with folded arms and eyes fastened upon the gunner. Not a word was spoken and in the almost deathly silence an officer lowered the state flag which flew at the front of the building and raised the stars and stripes. Soldiers poured through the Camp Street gate which opened on the river front while the crowd, suddenly finding its voice, shouted their praise of the Mayor.

The officer in charge spoke to the Mayor and they went inside to the Mayor's office to confer upon the order to surrender.

In the meantime William and the other boys, spurred by Diana's scorn, went to the mint. The crowd had dispersed and there were only a few stragglers when they arrived. The boys stood there looking with grave eyes at the flag flying from the flagpole. They had once loved that flag and would have been willing to lay down their lives in its defense. Even now it seemed almost a desecration to do the thing they contemplated, but when they remembered the desecration of their own Confederate flag, their anger spurred them on to the dangerous deed.

"Who's going to take it down?" one of them asked.

They would not admit that they were afraid, but each one knew the danger and what the consequences might be.

"I'm going to do it," William declared.

The thought of Diana's praise for what he was about to do spurred him on and gave him courage. Perhaps she would care for him a little when he told her that he had done it because of her. While the others stood watching in silence, he untied the rope that held the flag and lowered it, then tore it from the rope and rolled it into a bundle.

"What're we going to do with it?" one of them asked.

"Let's take it and give it back to the Yankees," another suggested.

"That's a good idea," William agreed. "Come on, fellows, let's go and throw it back in their faces."

It was not difficult to find where the soldiers had gone, for people were still going toward the City Hall, following in the wake of the soldiers. The boys arrived there just as the state flag had been lowered and the Mayor and several soldiers had gone inside. Through the open window the boys could see the Union soldiers and the Mayor standing in a group nearby.

Acting upon impulse, William made his way through the crowd until he was under the window and then he threw the flag inside. He turned and was lost in the crowd before the soldiers on guard at the entrance saw what had happened. He and his companions disappeared quickly, making their way through the crowd and going down a side street. Once out of sight of the mob, they ran as fast as they could. They separated at the suggestion of one of them. William returned to the Wilborn home and rang the bell, eagerly waiting to tell Diana the news.

Alicia answered the bell and ushered him into the living room while she went in search of Diana. Diana came in reluctantly, dreading to meet William. After her father's rebuke and after she had had time to think of what she had done, she realized how foolish and heartless she had been to suggest such a rash act. It could do no one any good and might endanger the safety of all of them. She greeted William with a grave face.

"Well, we did it," he announced triumphantly.

He was bubbling over with excitement. Now that the deed was done and he was in her presence, he felt like a hero. He had carried out the request of his lady and he was waiting for her smile of approval. Instead of a smile she looked at him solemnly.

"You mean that you really tore the flag down?" she asked.

"We sure did. We rolled that old flag up in a bundle and threw it right back at the feet of those Yankees there in the City Hall."

His eyes were shining and his face was eager and glowing.

"Who took it down?" she asked.

"I did." He spoke proudly. The fear and the dread of the possible consequences had left him. He was revelling in the bravery of his foolish act. "The other fellows got scared when we got down there, so I did it myself. Wasn't that the way you wanted it?"

Some of his exuberance left him as he saw her grave eyes fastened upon him. There was no light of approval in them and no smile of approval upon her face.

"I'm sorry you did it," she told him. "You shouldn't have done it."

"But you told us to!" he exclaimed, baffled by her change of attitude. "You almost accused us of being cowards when we hesitated about doing it."

"I know and I'm sorry I urged you to do it," she admitted. "Father made me see how foolish it was and how dangerous. I hope they don't find out who did it. You'd better go home and stay there until affairs are settled here. I'm sorry, William, if I've gotten you into any trouble."

"Sorry!" he ejaculated, disappointed and disheartened at her reaction to his news. His fear returned as he realized the seriousness of his rash act. He turned and left her without a word.

She stood where he had left her until she heard the door slam behind him, then she went to her room. She shut the door, then threw herself across the bed while she wept silently. She knew that tears could not atone for the foolish thing she had done, but she wept nevertheless, for her whole world seemed to have been shattered about her and her tears were for herself as well as for what she had done to William. Life which had seemed wonderful such a short time ago, now seemed drained of all happiness and the future was something which she did not dare to face.

17

GENERAL BENJAMIN BUTLER TOOK POSSESSION of the city with fifteen thousand men and the city was subjected to a reign of terror such as no one could have dreamed in a day of civilized warfare. Years before, the inhabitants had suffered indignities under the heel of O'Reilly, the governor under Spanish dominion, but he had never subjected the conquered inhabitants to such terror and sufferings as this Union general inflicted upon the people.

He came in with regiments marching to the strains of martial music. Crowds of Negroes lined the streets as the soldiers passed by. They shouted "We're free now and we're equal to the white folks!" They thought that emancipation had come with the arrival of the Union soldiers. The white citizens remained indoors, hoping for the best in this time of occupation, but soon to be made aware that the worst had befallen them.

Nowhere else in the battle zone of the nation did the conquered people suffer as the citizens of New Orleans were made to suffer during the brief period of this man's reign of terror. White citizens were subjected to every indignity possible. Negro soldiers who had grown brutal through the horrors of war were placed as guards at the homes of those supposed to be suspect. Houses were searched and valuables were taken under the pretense that they were the confiscated spoils of war. Silverware and jewelry and other valuables were stolen and sold for a pittance at public auction. If any protested, he was arrested. Sixty of the most prominent citizens were sent to Ship Island where they were put to work filling sandbags while Negro soldiers were put over them.

Butler had not been there long before he received his nickname of "Beast Butler." He was also called "Silver Spoon Butler" because of the silver he had had stolen. O'Reilly had been called "Bloody O'Reilly" when he executed some of the leading citizens, but "Beast Butler" was even worse.

Butler did not spare the ministry. Pastors were arrested because they did not pray for President Lincoln. A woman was arrested for laughing when the funeral procession of a Federal boatman passed by.

Under Butler's orders Federal officers were housed in the homes of prominent citizens to spy upon them as well as be fed and housed comfortably, instead of being placed in the barracks or less comfortable quarters.

One morning quite early the door bell rang at the Wilborn home and Diana, who was just coming downstairs, answered it. Roger was close behind, for he had cautioned them to be careful about letting anyone in. When the door was opened she uttered an amazed cry, for standing there, tall and handsome in his blue uniform, was Keith. Behind him was an orderly with his baggage.

She stared at him speechless while Keith surreptitiously put a finger to his lips and warned her with his eyes to keep silent.

"What does this mean?" she demanded, eyeing him coldly. She was wise enough not to call his name, for she understood his warning.

"It means that I am to be billeted here for the duration of the occupation," he said in crisp formal tones, then turning to the orderly he said, "Put the things inside the door and then you may go."

The orderly obeyed and left them. When Keith was sure that he was out of earshot, he turned back to the two at the door.

"I'm sorry to have to impose myself upon you," he told them diffidently, "but if I didn't come here, someone else would have come and I was afraid of what you might be subjected to. I'm here under orders, or I would not have dared to come. Believe me, I am doing this for your protection."

"What kind of protection can we expect from one of that beastly Yankee's men?" Diana cried angrily. "We may expect anything from him and his soldiers. They're worse than savages."

"I'll come inside, if you don't mind," he said as he went inside without waiting for their reply. "There might be someone spying upon me," he told them when the door was shut. "I don't want to put suspicion in anyone's mind or you might suffer from it. Please don't judge the rest of the Union army by the one in command here now. Many of us don't agree with what he is doing, but we are under his command and we must obey his orders or suffer the consequences. When he ordered us to find a place in the homes of the citizens, I came here as quickly as I could, for I want to protect you. It's the least I can do in return for all you have done for me."

"Why not go to the Mayhews?" Diana asked. "They are your friends also."

"Someone else is there. He is a friend of mine and he will not let any harm come to them. His two brothers are fighting in the Confederate army."

"You may occupy the guest room at the head of the stairs," Roger told him. "I'll help you carry your luggage up."

They went upstairs while Diana stood watching them. She had not yet recovered from the shock of seeing him and she was torn between mingled emotions. She was thrilled at the sight of him even though he wore the uniform which she hated. She was overjoyed to see that he had not been wounded, that he was still alive and as handsome as ever, but she was indignant that he should be thrust upon them in this manner and that they would have to sit at the table with him while he was wearing the enemy uniform. She determined that she would ignore him as completely as possible, yet she knew that she did not want to ignore him. She wanted to be held in his arms again and to feel the touch of his lips upon hers again, yet she felt that even this thought was treason to her Southland.

As soon as Keith had been established in his room he told Roger to hide everything of value that could be hidden. Their house had escaped searching thus far, but he knew that it might not escape, even though he was established there. The family silver was quickly disposed of in the basement while the jewelry was hidden in the attic. During this activity Diana held herself aloof. Angela accepted him as a friend and tried to make him feel less constrained and uncomfortable and Roger and Alicia did likewise, but Diana refused even to try to be friendly. At the table she refused to talk except in answer to some question and when the meal was finished, she excused herself and went to her room until Keith had left.

One afternoon he came in earlier than usual and found her in the living room alone. He hesitated a moment in the doorway, wondering whether or not he should try to talk to her. She looked up and saw him and the cold hostile light came into her eyes.

"I've been wanting to talk to you for some time, Diana," he said as he entered and sat down nearby.

"What is there for us to talk about? Nothing, so far as I know," she replied.

"There is much to talk about," he insisted. "You're making it very difficult for me when I have come here to try to make it a little easier for you and your family."

She laughed bitterly. "By compelling us to feed you when food is getting scarce and by compelling us to accept you when you have thrust yourself upon us."

He looked at her gravely and shook his head.

"That remark is unworthy of you, Diana. You have said many harsh things to me and have given me many insults, but I believe this is the worst. I know you were taught to be polite, but I fear that your hatred has made you forget what you were taught."

She colored and lowered her eyes as she said, "Is it impolite to speak the truth to an enemy?"

Her eyes suddenly flashed fire as she raised them and met his serious gaze.

"But I'm not an enemy and you know it. I came here under orders or I would not be here. If I had not come, someone else would have come to live with you and from what I have heard from others, you would have been subjected to all of the indignities which you have escaped. You would be treated as captives of war. And as for food, your mother would have been compelled to serve lavish meals from a dwindling larder. I came here to save you all of this because I love you and your family and I didn't want to see you suffer. I did it because I love you, Diana, and because I wanted to save you first of all."

"Love!" she ejaculated scornfully. "The kind of love you have for me is an insult, as I told you before."

"The love I have for you is no insult," he said quietly. "It comes from my heart and I fear that it will always be there. Why I love you I have never been able to understand. You have the capacity for sweetness and gentleness, but you have never given your better nature a chance to reveal itself. For me you have had only scorn and bitterness and insults. I realize that I'm a fool to keep on loving you when I know that I should not, but it is there in my heart and I don't have the power to remove it. Perhaps one day God will answer my prayers for you and you will accept Jesus as your Saviour and then all the sweetness which I long to see will be there in your new nature. That would make me happy beyond words."

"I have no desire to change my nature," she announced while her eyes smoldered wrathfully. "And don't ever speak to me of love as long as you wear that uniform!" Her voice rose wrathfully. "I will consider it an added insult to your being here while you are wearing it."

She rose and left the room. He sat there looking after her and a sigh escaped him. Salvation for her seemed utterly impossible, yet he knew that with God nothing was impossible. He went to his room with a heavy heart and feet that dragged as he mounted the steps. When he passed Diana's door he thought he heard the sound of sobs, but he could not be sure. Was she crying, he wondered. He hoped she was, for if she was, then he knew that what she had said and how she had acted had not been the real indication of what she felt. He knew that beneath that vanity and heartlessness, there must be something as lovely as her beautiful face, but he also knew that no one but God could bring it forth through the new nature which would be hers if she should ever let God have His way in her life.

While houses were being ransacked and valuables and silver were being stolen by soldiers under Butler's orders, women and children stayed off the streets. The French Market was almost deserted and food became more scarce. Farmers were afraid to bring their produce to the city, for if it was not commandeered by Butler's men, there were few who could afford to buy. The city was in a state of siege and some were in actual want. Churches were closed when some of the pastors had been arrested, for the members were afraid of being arrested for infringing upon some of Butler's orders.

Keith could not understand how such an uncouth, brutal man could have been put in command. Someone somewhere had surely made a mistake. He was yet to learn of Sherman's march to the sea through Georgia. War had its horrors of every description and innocent ones were perhaps the greatest sufferers.

William remained at home in obedience to Diana's warning. Now that he had had time to think over what he had done, he feared for what would happen to him, for he knew that Butler did not know the meaning of mercy. His fears were soon realized, for someone had told Butler that he had been the one who had torn down the flag.

One evening soldiers came to the small house where he and his mother lived and William was arrested. Butler declared that he would be hanged.

The news spread quickly and the next day brought consternation to all, especially to the Wilborn family. For once in her life Diana had to face the consequences of her foolish act. She was horrified and stricken with remorse and terror at the thought of what would happen to William. She had never dreamed that this could happen.

Men of prominence went to Butler to intercede for William and to beg for clemency. They stressed the boy's youth and the impetuosity that would naturally sway them in this time of stress and excitement and they argued that the city had not yet surrendered when the deed was done, so that, legally, he could not be accused of committing a crime against the occupying army. Butler cared nothing for the legality of his decree. He wanted vengeance and he was adamant against their pleas.

Diana was desperate. She knew that if William was hanged, his life would be lost because of her. She was responsible for what he had done. If he had not loved her he would not have done what she urged him to do. For the first time in her life she condemned herself, for she knew how guilty she was. In her desperation she went to Keith in the hope that he might do something to save the boy from such a horrible fate.

"I'm sorry I've been so rude and hateful to you," she began. "Please forgive me and do something to help me save William. I can't bear it if he should be hanged. Can't you try to save him?"

Keith looked at her sadly as he said, "I'm afraid there is nothing I can do. Butler won't listen to anyone when he makes up his mind to do anything. If I should go to him and try to persuade him to save the boy, he might get suspicious of me and you would suffer because I am here."

"Then you won't do anything?"

"I can't. I've told you why. I know what it would mean for you and your family. You've been safe this far because he knows I'm here to spy upon you and to see that you commit no treasonable act. He must not know that William is your friend. I wish there was something that I could do, but there is nothing."

"But I'm responsible for all this trouble," Diana cried. Tears coursed down her face. "I was the one who taunted him to tear down that flag. I accused those boys of being afraid and William did it because he loved me and wanted to please me. I can't stand by and see him hanged for something that I'm to blame for. Surely there is someone who can persuade Butler to have mercy and spare his life."

"All the influential men of the city have tried and failed. Even one of his officers tried to show him that he would only stir up trouble if the boy was hanged, but he would not listen. He wants to make an example of William."

"And all my life I shall feel like his murderer," she moaned.

"I'm terribly sorry," Keith murmured.

He longed to take her in his arms and wipe her tears away and try to comfort her but he dared not.

She dashed the tears from her eyes and raised her head defiantly.

"Then I'll go to Butler myself! I shall tell him the truth. Perhaps he'll listen to me. But I'm not going to stand by and let that boy be killed if I can save him."

She turned toward the door but Keith caught her arm and held her.

"Diana, please don't go to see Butler now. Wait a while."

He was hoping that Alicia or Roger would come in and prevent her from going.

"Why should I wait? If I do, it may be too late. I'm going now. Let me go."

He tried to plead with her but she would not listen. He let her go reluctantly and she went to her room. She returned presently while he waited anxiously, hoping that Alicia or Roger would come. She was no longer the weeping, desperate girl he had seen such a short while before. She was completely transformed. She had on a becoming street dress and a small hat was perched at a most becoming angle upon her dark curls. Her eyes were bright with the light of determination and no longer deluged with tears.

"Please don't go, Diana," Keith begged. "You'll only bring trouble on yourself and your family and you won't accomplish a thing."

"We shall see," she retorted as she swept past him and out of the door.

Keith wondered where Alicia was, but it was too late to hunt for her now. Roger had gone to the plantation early that morning. He could do nothing but wait anxiously for her return.

Diana tried to calm her fears as she neared Butler's headquarters. She was ushered into his presence without delay. When Butler was told that a beautiful young lady wished to see him, he ordered her admitted at once. When she faced him she had difficulty in giving him a forced smile, for fierce hatred rose within her when she remembered what her people had suffered under him and the fate that awaited William.

Butler leered at her for a moment, then spoke gruffly without asking her to be seated.

"What is it you want?" he asked. "If you came here about that scallawag Mumford, you're wasting your time. I've been bothered enough already about him. He hangs tomorrow, so state your business and be quick about it."

"I have come to plead for his life," she told him.

Fear mounted within her when she heard the dreadful news that William had so little time left, but desperation overcame her fear.

"You're wasting my time, so you'd better go," he said gruffly.

"Please have patience and listen to me, General," she begged in her most melodious voice, while her eyes looked pleadingly into his gross face. "He's so young and he did it when everyone was so excited and so stirred that they were not accountable for what they were doing. And you were not in command here then, so it wasn't done against you. Won't you please have mercy and spare his life? He hasn't harmed anyone."

"He's committed an act of treason and he shall die for it," Butler declared. "You may just as well save your breath and not take up any more of my time. I have no patience with you rebels."

Her anger almost boiled over, but she managed to appear calm and unruffled, for the situation was so terribly desperate.

"General Butler, please listen to me for a moment longer. William Mumford is not the guilty one. He would never have thought of tearing down that flag if I had not urged him to do it. I accused him of being afraid to do it and he did it to please me. We have known each other since childhood and he thought a lot of me. I'm the guilty one, not he. Please have mercy and spare him."

Butler looked her over in a way that made her blush, then he remarked, "In that case you should both hang. Then there would be two rebels less to reckon with."

In spite of herself, she recoiled at his words. Her eyes were wide with fright and she stared silently at him. He uttered a short laugh.

"You're not so brave after all, are you? When the rope stares you in the face, words die in your throat. See that sign up there?"

She turned and read the sign he indicated. "The venom of the she-adder is as dangerous as that of the he-adder."

The sign was typical of the man, as coarse and disgusting as he was.

"What do you think of that?" he asked with a leer.

"I have nothing to say," she told him, trying to control her anger.

She knew that she could expect no mercy from him and that William was doomed. She wished she had a gun! She'd shoot him where he sat and she would be glad that she had!

"Then you'd better go," Butler told her. "You've had your say. Just be glad that that pretty neck of yours won't be stretched tomorrow when that boy hangs. You should be there to see him hang, if it was you who made him commit his crime. It would be a lesson to you for the future."

She faced him while her eyes flashed fire. Uncontrollable anger made her throw caution to the winds.

"You deserve the name they've given you!" she cried. "You're ten times worse than the man they called 'Bloody O'Reilly!' You are a beast. The name 'Beast Butler' suits you well. I hope some day that you'll dangle at the end of a rope as you deserve!"

She turned to go, but Butler called an orderly standing at the door.

"Arrest this girl," he ordered. "Take her to jail and see that she doesn't have any communication with anyone. She'll go on the next boat to Ship Island. By the time she gets back, she'll learn to keep a civil tongue in her head."

The soldier took her by the arm to lead her from the room.

Take your filthy hands off of me!" she cried and jerked herself free. "I can go without being dragged like a common criminal by riff raff like you."

The soldier hesitated a moment, then led the way from the room. Diana followed with her head held high and skirts swishing about her small feet. She passed outside to the echo of Butler's brutal laughter.

Keith waited nervously for Diana to return. He knew only too well the danger she was in but he knew that there was nothing he could do. Above all things he did not want Butler to know that he was a friend of the family. Not for his sake, but for theirs. He began to pace the floor nervously and anxiously. Presently Alicia came in and found him there.

"What's the matter?" she asked, knowing that something was wrong.

"How I wish you had been here sooner!" Keith exclaimed. "Perhaps you could have stopped her. Diana has gone to Butler to intercede for William's life. She has been gone for almost two hours and I'm afraid to think of what might have happened to her."

"Why did you let her go?" Alicia asked. "Why did you?" Her voice was accusing.

"I couldn't stop her. I tried to. I didn't know where you were. I knew that Mr. Wilborn had left town this morning. She feels that she is responsible for William's danger. Since others have failed to move Butler, she hoped that she would be able to persuade him to be merciful."

"No one could persuade that man to show mercy," Alicia remarked bitterly. "We must do something to find out what has happened to her. Can't you go to Butler and find out? Perhaps she didn't get to see him. At least we must find out where she is."

"Please don't think me a coward for not offering to go to

General Butler," he begged. "But if I go to him to ask about her, Butler will be suspicious of me. If he finds out that I am her friend, he'll remove me from here and someone else will be put here in my place. If Diana has been to see him, he will regard all of you as enemies and I fear that you will be subjected to every indignity possible under the espionage of some other soldier if I am taken away from here. I know only too well what has happened to others."

"Then I'll go myself, if you're afraid," she declared distractedly.

Keith was surprised and hurt by her words and the look she gave him. He had never heard her speak in this tone before. She had always been so gentle and considerate of everyone. He knew that it was because she was so emotionally upset and had cause to be.

"I'll go, if that is what you want, but believe me, it will only bring more trouble than you've already had," he told her.

He was on his way to the door when Roger came in. Alicia told him what had happened. She began to cry and he took her in his arms while he spoke to Keith.

"I don't think you should go to Butler," he said. "I am the logical one to go. If anyone is to suffer for whatever rash act Diana might have committed, it should be I. Surely he can't blame a father for wanting to know what has happened to his daughter."

He left the house at once and hurried to Butler's headquarters. He was stopped at the door by a sentry who informed him that Butler had left his office and would not return that day.

"What do you want with the General?" the sentry asked.

"I wanted to ask him if my daughter had been to see him. She was on her way here this afternoon and she has not come home and we are worried about her."

The soldier uttered a short laugh as he said, "You should be worried, if she's the girl who came here this afternoon to beg for that fellow's life who's going to be hanged tomorrow. She's in jail for insulting the general."

Stunned and desperate, Roger went at once to the jail

and asked for permission to see Diana. He was told that Butler had given orders that no one should be allowed to communicate with her until after the execution. Sick at heart and desperately afraid for Diana, he could do nothing but return home with the tragic news.

Alicia wept quietly in his arms when he returned and told them what had happened. Angela went at once to Mammy's room in the servants' quarters at the back of the house.

"Please pray with me, Mammy," she said when she had told the old slave what had happened. "I just don't seem to be able to pray myself. What's going to happen to William and what might happen to Diana is so terrible."

"I sho' will, chile," Mammy said. "I jes' cain't understand why dat chile don' let de Lawd save her po' li'l soul. She done got Marse William into trouble and now she done got herself in a fix too. Ain't no one but de Lawd kin do nothin' fo' her."

Together they prayed while Angela knelt at Mammy's side with the old Negro's arm around her. They prayed that if it were God's will William's life might be spared and that Diana might be saved from her own folly and that she might yield her life to the Lord.

Angela realized the next day, with growing horror and a heart torn with grief, that God had not seen fit to answer their prayers for William. Perhaps, she thought, they had not prayed earnestly enough or soon enough, but she believed, even in this dark hour, that God's ways were always best, even though she might not be able to understand.

Night came and in his narrow cell William waited for what would take place the next day. One of the soldiers on guard had told him brutally that when morning came, his neck would be stretched at the end of a rope. He knew that he had only a few hours of life left. He paced the floor of his cramped quarters until he was exhausted and then sank upon the bunk with his head in his hands.

He tried to think, but thoughts crowded into his agonized brain while mental pictures of the past raced through like a fast run motion picture. He looked back into his young life and saw those who had been near and dear to him. He saw Angela when they were childhood sweethearts and he remembered how she had tried timidly, yet so earnestly, to speak to him about his soul and the importance of salvation. He had either brushed her off or had laughed at her attempts to make him surrender his life as she had done. How he wished that he had listened to her then! Now it was too late. He was on the brink of eternity and he was desperately afraid.

He wanted to pray, but he did not know how to pray. He couldn't remember ever having prayed. His mother was not a Christian and had gone to church only rarely before the tragedy which unsettled her mind. He thought of his mother and tears came, though he tried to restrain them. She would be utterly alone and she needed him very much. Who would look after her and try to comfort her when those spells of depression came?

He lay upon the bunk and buried his face in the pillow while sobs shook him. He reached out in the darkness of despair, but there was no helping hand to uplift him and give him courage. He would die with terror in his heart and utter darkness within his soul. If he could only talk to Angela and have her pray with him! She would comfort him and give him the help he needed in this dark hour. But it was too late. He had refused to listen and he had forsaken her for Diana when he knew that Angela had given him the first love of her girlish heart.

His thoughts turned to Diana. What a terrible thing she had done to him! How she had let him down when he had had such high hopes that she would care more for him when he had done her bidding. She had not even come near him since his arrest. She was afraid of what might happen to her. How selfish and vain she was! How different from Angela. How could he ever have turned from Angela to her? He did not know that no one had been allowed to see him nor that Diana was not far away, prisoner herself because she had tried at last to atone for her foolish deed.

He could not sleep, even though he was spent and worn, and when morning came he was weak and shaky, but when they came for him he stood upon his feet and held his head high, even though his heart was beating against his ribs with the agonizing thud of terror. He would not let these Yankees know how terrified he was, how his whole soul quailed before the imminence of eternity. They would never know that he was looking into a future that was dark and full of horror, for it was without the least ray of hope. He had been deaf to a young girl's pleading to give his life to God and now he was going into a vast unknown where he would be cut off from God forever, where he could never know the peace and security which Angela had tried to make him accept.

He heard the slow, solemn beat of drums as the soldiers came to form the guard that would lead him to the place of execution. Butler was taking no chances of any demonstration or attempt to liberate his prisoner. He was determined that this boy should be hanged as an example to these rebels and a reminder of what would happen to them, if they disobeyed his orders.

With a Macabre sense of humor, he had decided that young Mumford should hang from the flagpole from which he had torn the Union flag.

The soldiers marched him to the mint to the rhythm of drumbeats and took their places in serried ranks at every intersection, guarding every approach to the place of execution. William marched in their midst with head held high and eyes straight ahead, walking erect and displaying a courage that belied the terror within. His knees shook so that he could scarcely walk, but he controlled his weakness, so that no eye that beheld him could see beneath the pallor of his face the blackness of despair within his heart.

He stood erect when he was led to the spot from which the rope dangled. He felt the roughness of the rope as it was slipped over his head and about his neck. There was a bugle blast and his body went hurtling into space, then dangled limply beneath the very flag which he had torn from its place, but which was now waving gently in the breeze, the stars and stripes, the red and blue and white, flaunting their colors over his lifeless body.

The soldiers marched away to the thud of drumbeats while the body was lowered and turned over to the mother whose mind had already been affected by the death of her husband.

18

DIANA WAS DAZED WITH SHOCK at the suddenness of her arrest. At first she couldn't believe that it was really true. This must be some horrible nightmare. Soon she would waken and find herself safe at home. But when night came on, after she had sat numb and stricken upon the bunk in the dirty prison cell, despair took possession of her. She wished that she had listened to Keith. He had warned her of what might happen if she went to Butler and now it had happened and it was worse than either of them had thought. She was afraid to think of what might happen next. She knew that she could expect the worst from Butler. She wondered if he really meant to send her to Ship Island or if he had only been trying to frighten her. The thought of being sent there made her shudder. Word had come back from some of the prisoners there. They had to work in the hot sun from morning to night, filling sandbags, while Negro soldiers stood over them urging them to more speed. They couldn't imagine why these sandbags should be needed. One of the men who had been sent there was sent home to die and he said that living conditions on that hot, sandy island were unspeakable.

She longed for Angela. Not until now did she realize how dear her younger sister was. She wanted her more now than she did her mother. Angela could comfort her in this hour even better than her mother could. She remembered how cross she had been with Angela when Angela had teased her and how scornful she had been of Angela's faith and faithfulness to what she believed. She longed for the peace which Angela possessed, for she was listening at last to the accusing voice of conscience and it brought torture.

She tried not to think of William. He must be in this same prison. He would die tomorrow and she would be to blame for his death. All the rest of her life she would carry the burden of that thought, that she was his murderer, as much as if she had killed him with her own hand. Remorse tore at her and she threw herself upon the bunk and wept long and bitterly. She tried to sleep but sleep would not come. She could not forget that last scene with William. He had come to her in such high spirits, telling her that the deed had been done and waiting with anticipation for her smile of commendation. And she had failed him. She had put fear in his heart and had sent him away to hide and to be arrested and condemned to die.

She could not forget that look on his face when he had left her. He had looked so crestfallen and disappointed and hurt. His shoulders had slumped and his feet dragged as he walked away. She could never forget that as long as she lived.

The next morning a guard brought her breakfast but when she took one look at it she could not eat. She was not hungry, but if she had been, the sight of that dirty pan with the greasy food was enough to destroy her appetite. Presently she heard the muffled sound of drums and she knew that they were taking William away. She would never again see his wistful eyes following her while she talked and flirted with some other boy. She would never again hear his boyishly stammering words as he tried to tell her of his love and to beg her to give him a little hope that she could care for him. She covered her ears to shut out the sound of those drums, but they seemed to penetrate to the very depths of her soul and she felt like shrieking to them to stop, that it wasn't fair to cut off a young boy's life for one rash act, committed because he loved a girl who wasn't worthy.

For the first time in her selfish life, she realized what she had done to so many hearts. Not all of them would suffer as William would suffer, but she knew that she had destroyed something in many of them, their trust and faith in a girl who was not worthy of either.

She heard the faint echo of a bugle blast on the still morning air, for this morning there was no one upon the streets, no carts rattling by, no people hurrying to their work. The city was wrapped in a cloak of silence. It was their protest against this merciless act of brutality. After an interval there came the faint echo of drumbeats once more. It was over. William was gone. And from now on she would never know peace again.

The city watched behind closed shutters as the funeral procession made its way to the cemetery. The bereft mother was accompanied by a few sympathetic friends who were brave enough to dare Butler's anger, for they would not let her go to the grave all alone. Angela was in that number. She could not stay away, even though she knew that she also might be arrested for showing her friendship to the criminal's mother.

Angela seemed to be able to comfort the grieving and demented woman as no one else had been able to do. Though Mrs. Mumford did not have enough mind to understand just what Angela was telling her about the peace of God that He alone could give in a time like this, the girl's gentle, soothing voice seemed to bring calm to her troubled mind. She clung to Angela through the brief service at the grave. Butler had not placed any restrictions upon the funeral proceedings. Now that his vengeance had been completed, he was willing to forget the affair.

After the funeral Angela went home with Mrs. Mumford and tried to persuade her to eat something, but the bereaved mother would not eat nor would she respond to Angela's efforts to converse with her.

She moaned and called pitifully for William. Her mind had gone back to the past when William was a little fellow. The present with its tragedy had been blotted out.

"William! Don't run away and hide from me," she called. "I promise you I won't whip you. Come on back home, William. I need you. William! William! Where are you?"

The pitiful cry continued at intervals. In spite of Angela's efforts to prevent her, she went out upon the street and wandered through the dusk, calling for her son. Sick at heart, Angela went home, for she knew that there was nothing that she could do. Neighbors had promised to do what they could for her.

The next day Roger went to see Butler. This time he was admitted to Butler's office. Butler listened with cold indifference to his plea for mercy for Diana.

"Why should you expect me to be more lenient with your daughter than to any other rebel who has committed a crime?" he asked.

"But she has not committed any crime," Roger expostulated.

"She told me that she was responsible for what that fellow did. She said she urged him to tear the flag down. Why shouldn't she be punished when she's as guilty as he was? You should be grateful that I didn't hang her beside him. You rebels'll have to understand that the army of the United States is in command here and that you are under military rule under my authority, so you'd better act accordingly. I'll teach you if I have to hang every one of you."

Roger could scarcely control his anger as he looked into the malevolent eyes of the general who was such a disgrace to his title, but he spoke quietly.

"I'm sure you've had no cause for complaint since you took command here," he replied. "The deed for which young Mumford paid with his life was done before you took command and before the city had actually surrendered. Surely you can't hold a young girl guilty of treason because she spoke rashly in a time of turmoil when the whole city was in a state of excitement and perhaps no one was quite accountable for what he said or did. I beg of you to be merciful and to release her. She is so young and youth is always impetuous. Can't you understand that and pardon her for what she did?"

"When she's had time to learn her lesson, I'll consider pardoning her," Butler conceded while an evil smile hovered about his lips. "She shall have a little outing at Ship Island

where perhaps the breeze from the Gulf may wipe away the
heat of impetuosity about which you speak so glibly."

"If you are determined not to pardon her, won't you let
me take her place? Send me there instead, I beg of you," Roger
pleaded distractedly.

"How would that teach her?" Butler demanded. "She is
the one who needs to learn to keep her tongue. Just let this be
a lesson to you and whatever friends you may have. You are a
defeated people and you may as well learn to act like it." He
turned to an orderly standing at the door. "Show this man
out," he said, then turned to his desk and began to write.

Roger went out seething with anger and torn with grief and
horror at the thought of what would happen to Diana. There
was nothing that he could do but return home with the heart-
breaking news. Others had interceded for William to no avail
and he knew that there was no one who might help him.
Butler was in command and though many of the soldiers under
him despised him for being the brute that he was, yet no one
had the power to disobey his orders.

Despair filled the hearts of those at home who waited for
the outcome of Roger's visit. Alicia and Angela burst into
tears when Roger told them that Butler was adamant and that
Diana would be sent to Ship Island. Keith was frantic, but he
could do nothing but hope and pray that in some way news
might reach headquarters of the Union forces and that Butler
would be replaced. Even that, however, wouldn't help Diana
now. He dreaded to think of what she would be called upon
to endure on that desolate, heat-scorched island. He felt that
Alicia blamed him for not trying to help. Her eyes seemed to
reproach him when they met his, though she said nothing. He
felt miserable and constrained whenever he was in the presence
of the family. He felt for the first time that he was an enemy
in their midst, or at least he thought this was the way they
felt about him. He spoke of this to Roger. Roger had been to
see Butler again and begged permission to see Diana, but even
this request had been refused. The four were plunged into
deeper depths of despair.

"I wish that I didn't have to remain here and force you to accept my presence," Keith told Roger, "for I feel that all three of you hate to have me around. I represent the man who has done this terrible thing to you. I'm sure that Mrs. Wilborn reproaches me for not trying to do something to help William and Diana, but I do hope that you understand my position. I trust that you believed me when I said that if I tried to speak to Butler it would only make matters worse."

"I understand perfectly," Roger assured him. "Now that I have had the chance to see just what he is, I know that no one could turn him from his brutal purpose."

"I would leave here if I could," Keith said, "and relieve you of my presence. It is embarrassing to me and I know that it is a strain upon the women, but if I leave, you will be worse off."

Roger put a hand affectionately upon his arm.

"Try not to feel constrained by being forced to remain here. I understand perfectly and I'm sure the women do, but they are so upset and heartbroken that they don't realize just how they are acting toward you. Just give them time and they will be able to get over the worst of this shock. I'm sure they love you as much as they ever did."

Keith had to be content with that, but the waiting was hard for them all.

Roger went a third time to Butler and asked permission to send Diana some clean clothes and some little toilet articles he was sure she wanted, but again Butler refused.

"She has clothes enough," he informed Roger. "You couldn't expect her to wear what you would send her. She's dressed like all the other prisoners. She'll learn to be satisfied with what she wears and what she eats or she will wish that she had."

"Would you mind telling me when she is to leave?" Roger asked.

Butler eyed him and that evil smile spread once more across his lips.

"She has already left. She left at dawn yesterday."

Roger did not break the news to the family until the next day. He did not have the courage to tell his wife until she had

had time to recover from this second disappointment. He merely told her that his request had been denied. When he did finally tell her, it was more than Alicia could stand and she collapsed. She was ill for several days and when she finally recovered sufficiently to be up again, she was a pitiful sight, pale and grief-stricken. When she tried to talk, she would begin to cry. Roger was afraid that she would have a complete nervous breakdown and he himself was distracted.

Angela, of them all, seemed to accept the situation with calmness. Though her eyes were often red from crying, no one saw her crying, and when they were together at the table or in the evening, she did her best to keep the conversation going and to spread a little cheer to lighten the gloom. One day when her mother had become stronger Angela took her to task for the way she was acting.

"Mother, I don't think you are casting your burden upon the Lord," she chided. "You're acting as if the Lord had forgotten you."

"I almost feel that He has," Alicia replied with a sigh. "If He hasn't, why has He let this happen to us? We have tried to serve Him faithfully. Surely we deserve something better than this."

"We have no right to question God's dealings with us, Mother," Angela reminded her. "We can't understand why some things happen, but I know that God still loves us and that He cares when things seem to go wrong. We should be thankful that we haven't suffered as much as others have in this terrible war, instead of moping and feeling that He has deserted us."

"What could be more terrible than to know that Diana is on that island with all those brutal soldiers?" Alicia demanded. "She might die there like Mr. Barker did. I can't bear to think of what may happen to her." Her tears began to fall.

"Can't you trust God to take care of her?" Angela asked gravely. "I love Diana as much as you do, Mother, but I'm trusting and praying that God will protect her and that out of all of this, everything will work together for good to us and to her."

Alicia turned upon her almost wrathfully and asked, "Did it work out that way for William?"

"No, it didn't," Angela admitted. "I can't understand why God didn't answer our prayers about him, but I still believe God's Word, even though I can't always understand why things happen like they do. Please try to cheer up, Mother, and trust God a little more. You were the one who taught me to trust Him and here I am having to beg you to trust Him."

Alicia smiled tremulously through her tears.

"I'm a pretty poor example of what a Christian should be, am I not? I feel rebuked, but I thank you for it, my darling."

She put her arms around Angela and they sat for a little while with their arms about each other. Then they prayed earnestly for the faith they sorely needed and for Diana's safety. After this Alicia was more cheerful and the atmosphere in the home was more like it was before tragedy laid its hands upon them. Each heart carried its burden of sorrow and anxiety, but everyone, even Mammy Sue, believed that God would take care of Diana and that one day she would be returned to them unharmed.

19

DIANA HOPED AGAINST HOPE that Butler would not send her to that dreadful prison camp on Ship Island. She spent the day of the execution in agonizing remorse and heartbreak over the death for which she felt responsible. She hoped that her father would come to see her and impart a little courage to her, but no one came except the prison guard with her food. She could not eat though she was beginning to feel weak from hunger. When night came again and she faced the long hours of darkness, she wondered how she would live through them, but finally she slept the sleep of exhaustion.

Early the next morning a slovenly woman brought her an

ill fitting dress in the drab color of the prevailing prison garb and told her to put it on.

"I won't wear that filthy thing," Diana declared with a return of her spirit. "I prefer to keep on my own clothes, even though they are all mussed and wrinkled."

"It ain't what you prefer," the woman told her with a twist of her lip. "It's what you're ordered to do. Wouldn't you be a pretty sight on Ship Island in those clothes?" She emitted a harsh laugh. "This dress is clean. I washed it myself."

"Ship Island!" Diana echoed in dismay. "Am I really going there?"

"You're goin' there tomorrow," the woman told her.

Diana knew that it was useless to try to refuse to obey Butler's orders, so she donned the prison garment which hung like a sack upon her slender body. The woman laughed loudly when she surveyed Diana.

"Ain't you the fine lady now!" she cried.

When the woman left Diana sank upon the bunk. She tried to control her sobs, for she knew that they would only unnerve her more, but she could not. She was overwhelmed with horror at the thought of what the future held in store for her. She wondered why no one from home had come to see her. She knew that they must know where she was, for Keith knew that she had gone to see Butler. She finally decided that this was just another one of Butler's cruelties. They must have tried to see her and he had refused to let them. She wondered if she would ever see them again. The thought brought a new flood of tears. She would be cut off from everyone she knew and loved and perhaps for as long as the war lasted. She realized how very much she loved her family, more than she had ever realized before. Until now she had merely accepted them and had been cross and unreasonable so many times. She promised herself that if she ever saw them again, she would remember and treat them differently.

The day passed with agonizing slowness, even though she dreaded the coming of another day. Hunger forced her to eat sparingly of the food at which she rebelled. Finally night came and she managed to sleep fitfully, though her sleep was filled with troubled dreams.

Early the next morning she was driven to the river where a schooner was waiting to take her and several other prisoners to the island. The trip was long and tedious, for the wind was shifting and not too strong and the journey which could have taken only a few hours by steamboat, took all day and part of the night. They were landed near midnight and taken at once to their quarters, a make-shift shack with crude bunks and only the bare necessities in each cell.

Diana had not seen another woman on the boat and she wondered if there were any other women on the island. She dreaded to think of what she would face if there were no others. She spent the rest of the night in sleepless tossing on the hard bunk.

Early the next morning the guard brought her a bowl of grits and watered milk. Hunger forced her to eat. When she had finished another soldier came and opened her cell door.

"Can you cook?" he asked, eying her with a look that brought the color to her face.

"No, I can't. I never have cooked," she told him.

She wished that she did know how to cook. That would be better than filling sandbags.

"Well, you can learn," he told her. "In the meantime, you can wash dishes and help in the kitchen. Come along with me."

She followed him across the white sand which was already growing hot under the morning sun. They came to the kitchen shack not far away and she saw two women inside busy about a large stove. They looked slovenly and unkempt and Diana pitied them. Then it smote her suddenly with the thought that before long she would be looking as neglected and unkempt as they, in fact, she might even be looking that way now.

One of the women looked up as Diana and the soldier entered. Her eyes were dull and hopeless and she looked haggard and desolate. She scarcely noticed Diana as the soldier remarked that they could either teach her to cook or else let her clean pots and wash dishes.

After he had left Diana stood waiting for the woman to tell her what to do. The woman looked at Diana again and then uttered an exclamation.

"You're Diana Wilborn!" she cried in surprise. "What brought you here? What crime did you commit against Beast Butler and his precious soldiers?"

Diana dreaded to tell her the truth, but she thought that perhaps she would find it out later, so she might just as well tell it herself.

"I talked too much," she said slowly. "I told Butler that I was to blame when William Mumford tore down the flag."

"What happened to the boy?" the woman asked.

"He was hanged a couple of days ago," Diana replied through stiff lips. "I tried to save him, but I only got myself into trouble."

"I didn't think that even Butler would do a thing like that!" the woman exclaimed. "But I should have known that he would do anything. He had me sent here because one of his spies heard me laugh when the funeral procession of a Yankee boatman passed by. I suppose he would have had me hanged if he had heard what I said. I said it was a pity that it wasn't Butler instead of one of his men. I'm Mrs. Meeker."

"I remember you now," Diana told her. "You were at the house one evening just before Butler came. You were with the Mayhews."

She never would have recognized the woman. In such a short time despair and hard work and poor food had done their worst and she was a wreck of her once formerly attractive self. Diana's heart sank to the depths as she realized that before this war was over, she would be looking like this woman.

"According to orders I'll have to let you clean up the kitchen until you can help us with the cooking, then we can share the work," Mrs. Meeker told her. "If we don't obey orders it will be just too bad. We can't expect mercy because we are women."

She introduced the other woman, Mrs. Fisher, to Diana and then she led Diana to the shelf where the dishpan and a stack of dirty dishes stood. Diana went to work washing dishes. She had never washed dishes before, nor had she ever used a broom and long before she had finished the dishes and swept the kitchen, her muscles ached and she thought she would drop from exhaustion, but she set her lips determinedly and finished the work without murmuring. She knew that she would have to make the best of the situation as the others were doing, but despair swept over her as the long days of the future loomed ahead of her, with no hope for release until the war should end — if she lived that long.

She had little time to rest between meals, for it was almost time to start the next meal before the dishes of the previous meal were stacked in their places. When night came she was glad to drop down upon her bunk and sleep the sleep of exhaustion.

Days passed with monotonous regularity until she lost count of time. Occasionally a new prisoner was brought over, but no one ever left the island. Summer passed and autumn came while winds became more threatening and waves beat higher upon the narrow sandy stretch of the island. A hurricane swept the island and blew down some of the shacks housing the troops. The winds were chill, making life more miserable for the poorly housed prisoners with their insufficient clothing and cover.

Back in the city Butler pursued his despotic control. The citizens had been whipped into outward submission, but inwardly they raged at his inhuman tactics. Keith and the others in the Wilborn household grew more anxious as the days passed and they could get no news of Diana. Alicia grew thin and pale with worry and grief, though she did her best to keep up her faith and to respond to Angela's efforts to cheer her through these grief-laden days.

September came and with it the blow which was to finally defeat the South and bring disaster and disorder for many months to come after the war ended. President Lincoln issued his emancipation proclamation. There was jubilation among the liberated slaves and there were some acts of reprisal against cruel masters who were reaping what they had sowed, while there was consternation and despair among the planters. The proclamation was the desperate act of a man who had the weight of a great responsibility upon his shoulders and who was doing his utmost to end the war as soon as possible, in order to save a nation from destruction and to prevent useless loss of lives.

Roger went to his plantation after the news had been spread across the front page of the paper in glaring headlines. He wanted to see what the result would be on his own place. He was confident that there would be no disorder, for his slaves had long been free. His confidence was justified, for he found everything just as he had left it not long before. Butler had allowed the plantation owners who lived in the city to visit their plantations in order to keep them going. He knew that if he did not, his own troops might feel the pinch of hunger.

Roger found the slaves going about their work as usual, singing as they worked in the fields of growing cane or working about their cabins in their small gardens. His overseer told him that the only reaction he had found when the news reached them was their joy that others who did not have the same happy situations as they had, would now be able to get out from under the yoke of their oppressors. One or two of the younger fellows had wandered away but he was sure they would come back. They did, just a few days later. They found that they were much better off with a roof over their heads and three meals a day than wandering around with no money and no job and little prospect of getting one.

Roger talked with a few of the Negroes and was satisfied that they were content to remain as they were. On his way back to town he offered a silent prayer of gratitude that he had been led by the Lord to do what was required of a Christian toward those who served him. On some plantations houses and barns had been burned by slaves before they fled to freedom.

Vicksburg was still under siege by General Grant and New

Orleans was cut off from the rest of the world. The war was dragging out its slaughter with no end in sight.

Diana and the others on Ship Island knew nothing of what was happening in the world outside and they felt forsaken by everyone. As the weeks passed and fall turned into winter, Diana wondered if they would ever live to see home again. Then at last came the news that caused joy and relief to the citizens of New Orleans. General Banks was sent to replace Butler, the beast of New Orleans.

Keith wondered if word had gotten to headquarters, but he never knew what had brought about the change in command. The citizens had been enslaved for so long that they did not dare to celebrate openly, but they met in homes to spend a time of rejoicing that their brutal tyrant had been relieved of his command and that they were free from his cruelties.

Order was restored out of the chaos of Butler's regime. Churches which had been closed for months were opened again, for now the pastors felt that they were free once more to worship and to preach with the liberty upon which their country was founded. Shops which had been closed because they were so often raided by soldiers, were opened and though their stocks were woefully depleted, people came to buy with their scanty supply of cash.

General Banks announced that the citizens would be treated with due respect to their rights as long as they did not commit any act of rebellion or disorder.

One morning while Diana was helping in the kitchen after breakfast, a ship arrived at the island. An officer came with the news that every prisoner was to be returned to his home at once. There was no excitement among the prisoners. A few of the older men shed surreptitious tears, but the others took the news quietly. They were dazed and could scarcely believe that liberty had come at last.

It was night when the boat reached the city and tied up at the dock. Diana was glad that it was dark, for she hated to face the world in the worn and ill fitting garment she was wearing. There were conveyances to take the refugees to their homes. Not until she was in the carriage and on her way to the home she had thought she would never see again, did tears come to her eyes, but she wiped them away swiftly.

Alicia and Roger were in the living room trying to read, but their thoughts were not on the books they held. Angela was at the piano softly playing a hymn that she loved. When the knock came they hesitated to answer it. They had not yet grown used to the new regime and they wondered what new danger threatened. When it came again Roger went to the door with the two women close behind him.

Roger opened the door and stared for a moment in amazement at the bedraggled figure standing there. Then he uttered a loud cry.

"Diana! Diana! Oh, thank God!"

She threw herself into his arms with a sob and he held her close while he wept unashamed with her. He led her into the living room when she had kissed her mother and Angela while their tears mingled as they cried for joy.

"How good God has been to give you back to us!" Alicia cried as she held her child close. "I've been so full of fear and doubt, but Angela has been a tower of strength to us all. Now I'm ashamed that I doubted so often. It's been terrible, hasn't it, darling?" she asked as Diana sat down beside her.

"Yes, it was," Diana sighed. "But just now I don't want to talk about it. I want to talk about you all. I've cried myself to sleep so many nights thinking of you and longing for you. I'll never be as cross and hateful again, I promise you. Where is Keith?" she asked presently. She was disappointed that he was not there. She had forgotten how unkempt she looked and how she had dreaded having him see her like this.

"He's not with us any longer," Alicia told her.

"Has he left the city?"

The others did not seem to notice her look of concern, but Angela saw and she was sure that what she had guessed before was true.

"No," Alicia said. "I think he's still here, but we haven't seen him since Butler left. General Banks ordered the soldiers to be housed in the barracks where they should have been all along. I suppose that Keith felt that he shouldn't come here now. He may be under orders to have no communication with us. We are enemies, you know," she reminded Diana.

They talked for a while but Diana was very tired and they decided to go to bed.

"How about a glass of milk and some cookies?" Alicia asked.

"It would be heavenly!" Diana exclaimed. "I haven't tasted real milk since I left here that dreadful day. What we had was more than half water. How have you managed cookies when I'm sure that everything is so scarce now?"

"That's my little secret," and Alicia gave her a smile. "We'll get along somehow until this dreadful war is over and I shall never complain again, now that I have you safe and sound at home again."

When they parted for the night the two girls went upstairs with their arms around each other.

"How good it will be to sleep in a real bed again!" Diana remarked as they came into her room. "Everything looks twice as beautiful as it did before." She turned to Angela and gave her a kiss. "I promise that I'll never be angry with you again when you tease me. I've wished for teasing a thousand times since I've been away."

Angela gave her a hug and smiled at her through her tears.

"I've reformed," she said. "I promise not to tease any more."

Diana sat at her dressing table and began to comb her dark hair. She gave a gasp as she looked at her sunburned face. It would take a long time for that suntan to fade and the creamy white skin to return to normal again. She sighed as she looked at her reflection.

"Don't sigh, sis," Angela admonished. "You're still the most beautiful of them all, even in that old rag. Shall I shut the door?"

"No. Leave it open. I never want the door between us to be shut again."

Angela wondered if their prayers for her salvation had been answered as their prayers for her return had been answered. When she looked in a few minutes later, wondering if she would see Diana on her knees, she was disappointed. Diana was already in bed and she had not prayed. Angela knelt by her own bed and prayed that, no matter what it took, Diana would yield her heart and her soul to the Lord. Little did she realize just what it would take before Diana did that.

20

FOR A WHILE AFTER DIANA'S RETURN she seemed to have changed. She could scarcely believe at first that she was free once more, that there were no more dirty dishes and pans to wash, no heavy broom to wield on a floor which seemed ever-lastingly filled with sand, and no hard bunk to torture her when she tried to sleep. Home had never seemed so dear and the garden had never looked so lovely, though most of the flowers had died when cold weather came.

As time passed, however, and the days came and went with monotonous regularity, she grew unhappy and discontented. For a time she had forgotten the chain of events which had sent her to Ship Island and the memory of William's death did not haunt her with its reproach. She had been too tired to think. But after the first thrill of her freedom had died down, she had time to remember and she became gloomy and despondent, much to the disappointment of the three who loved her.

"I was hoping she had changed," Angela remarked one morning to Mammy Sue while she helped the old colored woman string some beans for dinner. "I've prayed that all that she had been through would make her turn to the Lord for the comfort He could give her, but she's as far away from Him as ever."

"I guess it'll take more'n what she's been through to

change her," Mammy stated. "He gwine to have to whip her some mo' to make her see dat she cain't run away from Him when we's prayin' so ha'd fo' her to come to Him and be converted."

"She's still blaming herself for what happened to William. I don't believe she'll ever get over the horror of that."

"She ain't nevah gonna get oveh it until she asks de Lawd to fo'give her fo' what she did to dat boy. Ain't no good fo' her to grieve oveh it onless she asks de Lawd to fo'give her. An' it looks like she's got to take mo' whippin' f'm de Lawd befo' she do dat."

Diana came out just then and interrrupted their conversation.

"Isn't there anything more interesting to do around here than stringing beans?" she asked.

Her voice held the old note of discontent and Angela's heart sank.

"We could have a game of croquet," she suggested.

"How exciting that would be!" Diana retorted scornfully. "Are we allowed to go riding horseback or are we still deprived of all of our liberties?"

"I suppose we can, but I don't have any desire to ride. It's not the same since the Yankees came. Let's go in and have some music. We haven't played together for a long time."

"I haven't felt in the mood for music," Diana replied.

"Come on and get in the mood," Angela urged, taking her sister by the arm and leading her into the living room.

Diana longed to ask about Keith, but she did not want Angela to suspect that she was interested in him. Angela brought up the subject when they had played a few numbers.

"Keith used to like this piece, remember?" she said when they had finished it.

"Yes, now that you mention it," Diana replied with assumed indifference.

"I wonder where he is. It's strange that we haven't seen him since Butler left."

"Why should it be strange?" Diana wanted to know.

"When he didn't need us any longer, he just forgot us. After all, he is an enemy and we are nothing but a captured people, little more than prisoners. Why should he bother about us?"

"You know that's not the way Keith feels about us," Angela remonstrated. "We were his friends and I'm sure that he thought a great deal of us. There must be some reason why he hasn't been here. Perhaps he's been sent away."

Diana did not answer, but the thought that Keith might have gone to join in battle somewhere filled her with dismay.

The New Year dawned with little to cheer the hearts in the occupied city. The news that came from the war was not encouraging and the future looked dark indeed for the South. Grant was still hammering away at the forts upon the bluffs at Vicksburg and the city was still holding out valiantly, but the Confederates had met with disastrous defeats elsewhere.

A detachment of soldiers had reached the shores of Lake Pontchartrain and remained there, hemmed in on all sides by the Union army which was moving in from the East. Many of the soldiers were ill with malaria, but there were no medical supplies available. Their only hope was to get supplies from New Orleans just across the lake. One attempt had been made to contact someone in the city in order to get medical supplies, but the messenger who had volunteered to make the attempt had not returned and they were sure that he had been captured. This would make another attempt more difficult, for Banks would be on his guard against anyone else who tried to get through the lines. The Confederates determined, however, in desperation, to make another attempt. If this failed, the officer in command decided that they would have to surrender to Banks. This would be better than to let the men under him die for lack of medical care.

One evening Diana was sitting on the front porch. Angela and the others were in the living room. A man came through the gate and approached the house. She rose and waited for him to come nearer and to say what he wanted. He looked ragged and unkempt and she was still distrustful of everyone who was a stranger.

"I have a note for Miss Wilborn," the fellow said. "May I see her please?"

"I am Miss Wilborn," Diana informed him. "Let me have the note."

He fumbled inside his shirt and produced the note, much crumpled and dirty, and gave it to her.

"If you can do what the note requests, I'll be at the lake at dusk tomorrow night," he said and was gone before she could question him.

He had been so mysterious and seemed so nervous and apprehensive that she was just a little frightened as well as curious. She went to her room and opened the note.

"Darling," she read, "it has seemed an eternity since I last saw you. I never have had the chance to send you any word until now. Our men are dying and I am ill myself with malaria. We have no medicine and we need bandages and quinine and other supplies. I've written the list below. If you want to save the lives of all of us, please get these things and give them to the one who brought this note. He will tell you when to meet him. There is a light skiff that will be tied near the spot where we used to go for target shooting. You know the place. He will be there waiting for the supplies. I think the Union soldiers are guarding the lake front, so be careful, for our lives depend upon our getting these supplies. If we don't get them we will have to surrender and that will be terrible. God bless you and help you to get these things to us. I love you with all my heart. Ralph."

Ralph! She held the note in her hand while she stared at the signature. She had forgotten Ralph completely, for so much had happened since she had last seen him. But he loved her. How thrilling that thought was! How long it seemed since she had had any admirers hovering about her and waiting for her smile. And Ralph was still one of them, even though she had treated him so shamefully in the beginning. She remembered that he had forgiven her and she also remembered their last little moments together, when she had told him how much she treasured his friendship. She had thought then that his ardor had seemed to have cooled, but now she was sure that he still loved her.

Some of the joy of life returned to her in this moment. She looked at her reflection in the mirror and noted with satisfaction that she was still beautiful. The strain and weariness and near-starvation had not left any permanent marks to mar her beauty. She exulted in that.

She read the note over again. She knew the place Ralph had mentioned. They had gone there before war had separated them with the others in their group to practice target shooting. The memory of those carefree days brought a smile to her lips but as she read the note again and realized the seriousness of the situation, the smile disappeared.

She wondered what she could do to help those men over there on the other side of the lake, dying for lack of medical supplies. If she could do what Ralph had asked her to do, perhaps she would have helped to save the lives of many. It would help to remove the sting of remorse over the death of William. Perhaps if she could do this, she could have some peace of mind. Her eyes shone with the light of a great resolve.

She decided not to tell anyone about the note. She would get those supplies and take them to the lake herself. If no one else knew about this, then no one but herself would be blamed if she failed or if the messenger should be captured and taken to prison.

She made a list of the things Ralph had listed and then she hid the note and went down to the living room as if nothing momentous was about to happen.

That night she could not sleep, but tossed restlessly and waited for morning, for she had much to do and she must be careful not to arouse suspicion or curiosity.

After breakfast she told Angela that she was going out for a little walk. She hoped that she had enough money to pay for the supplies. If she did not, she would have to have them charged and that might arouse suspicion. She remembered that during Butler's despotism, druggists had been arrested for selling drugs to persons suspected of helping those in the Confederate army. She took her savings with her and hoped for the best.

She went to several drug stores and bought small quantities of the things she needed. She was afraid to buy everything at one store. She put the things into the large reticule she carried and returned home, tired, but satisfied that she had been successful in this part of her mission. The rest would be more difficult and dangerous, but she was determined to make the effort and hope for success.

"You must have had a long walk. You look tired," Angela remarked when she returned.

"I am," she admitted, "but it is good to be able to get out and walk until I get tired. I loved it."

She went to her room and arranged the purchases in two packages, after she was sure that Angela was busy in the back giving her dog a bath. She got out the pistol her father had given her. It was the one she had used when she had gone target shooting with Ralph and the others. She oiled it and loaded it. Her hands trembled with nervousness. She hoped that she would not have to use it, but she knew that she would if she should be forced to. She tried to conceal her nervousness from the family as the day passed and dusk approached and she hoped that they did not suspect the tension under which she waited for the time to come when she would meet that messenger.

She slipped out of the house and had her horse saddled, then she got her reticule and a dark cloak and the pistol. She led the horse out the side gate, hoping that none of the family would appear and ask questions. She sighed with relief when no one appeared. She rode slowly along the avenue with the precious supplies concealed beneath the voluminous folds of her dark riding habit. The pistol was in the pocket of the cloak.

She passed an occasional soldier and her heart beat faster, but none of them paid any attention to her and she felt relieved that she was not causing an suspicion. When she reached the suburbs of the city she rode a little faster, for she was anxious to get to the rendevouz and send her horse back home so that she could hide while waiting for the messenger to meet her. She hadn't thought how she would get home after she had delivered the supplies.

Just an hour or so before Diana left her home, General Banks was having an interview with Keith. When Keith had been removed from the Wilborn home he had left with regret, for he knew that he would not be able to get any news of Diana, except in a roundabout way, for orders had been given by the general that there should be no fraternizing between the soldiers and civilians.

"I have an idea that those Confederates will make another attempt to get supplies through our lines," the general told Keith. "I don't want them to get help, for when they become desperate, they will surrender and that's what I want. No use to waste men to cross the lake and fight them. I want you to pick enough of the men under you to picket the lake front from beyond the old Spanish Fort to the Manchac road. The road itself is always under guard, of course, but they may try again to cross the lake at its narrowest point. I leave the details with you."

"I shall do my best, sir," Keith told him. "I shall personally conduct the lineup of the men and remain on guard tonight to see that everything is done to protect the spot from runners with contraband."

The general smiled approval. "I knew I could depend upon you." The general had known Keith's father years before.

Keith picked his men carefully, choosing those he believed would stay awake through the night and not relax their vigilance, for the watching would get monotonous through the long hours. Then they left for the lake front. It would be difficult to guard the area, for there were stretches of swamp where cypress trees stood like grim ghosts between the old fort and the road to Manchac. It would be easy for someone to hide in the swamps until the sentries had passed.

It was almost dark when Diana reached the spot where she was to turn the precious supplies over to the messenger. She could see the dim outline of the skiff. She hid in a clump of bushes and waited nervously for the man to appear. As time passed and he did not come, she grew cold with fear, then she heard voices not far away, coming from the direction of the Spanish Fort.

"I think I see a skiff over there beyond that clump of cypress," someone said.

"We'll have to wade out and sink it," someone else said in muffled tones.

The voice sounded vaguely familiar to Diana but there was no time to waste thinking about familiar voices. She must not let them get to that skiff. She made a desperate decision and acted upon it, for there was no time to think of the possible consequences. That medicine must be gotten to those soldiers. Ralph was over there and he was depending upon her. If the messenger could not take them, she must. Perhaps he had already been captured and held prisoner.

She put the reticule over her shoulder under her cloak and got out her pistol. She did this by sheer instinct, without any clear idea of what she would do with the gun, but it gave her a measure of courage and a sense of protection. She slipped out from the protecting shadow of the trees and untied the skiff. She dropped the reticule into it and pushed it out a little ways from shore, then prepared to step in.

Just then someone called out from the darkness, "There's someone getting into that skiff!"

"Fire upon him!" came a sharp command from a voice nearby.

There was a blast from a gun but the shot missed her. Then someone nearer fired a pistol as he came sloshing through the marsh toward her. She saw his dim outline and she fired at him, then she climbed into the skiff. She felt a stinging pain in her leg and she knew that she had been hit. As she clambered into the boat and hastily took up the oars, she heard a groan. The man who had shot her had disappeared. More shots came from guns farther away, but she rowed desperately and the firing ceased as she disappeared into the darkness.

She was thankful that the lake was calm and she uttered

a silent prayer, scarcely conscious that she was praying, that the lake would remain calm until she had crossed it. Squalls often burst suddenly upon the treacherous lake and overturned small craft.

When the first excitement had died down within her, she realized the gravity of her situation. Enemy boats might be in pursuit. If they should overtake her, she would spend the rest of the war in prison. A worse fate might await her. She knew that she could expect the worst.

Though she had rowed frequently, she had never rowed for any length of time at a stretch. Never in her wildest dreams could she have pictured herself putting her skill at rowing into practice at a time like this and in such a situation. She had never dreamed that she would be thankful for those days of toil on Ship Island, when she wielded that heavy broom and lifted those heavy pots, but she knew now that her muscles were strong and firm because of that grueling exercise. Otherwise she could not have lasted a mile. The way was long, however, and she wondered if her strength would hold out.

Her leg began to throb and the blood trickled down and settled in her shoe. She could not stop yet to try to bandage it, for she feared pursuit, but as time passed and there was no sign of anyone following her, she stopped long enough to remove her stocking and to make a crude bandage with it and her handkerchief.

She became so weary as she toiled on that she thought she could not take another stroke. She stopped for a little while and rested on the oars, but she felt the boat drifting and she took up the oars again. She must not drift beyond the place where she hoped to find the Confederates' camp. She had no idea where that was, but she felt that it must be directly opposite from where she had started. Her strokes became weaker but she toiled doggedly on while her head began to swim and the pain in her leg increased. She wondered how many hours had passed and how far she had come, then wondering and thinking seemed to stop functioning and she became an automaton, rowing and struggling against overpowering weariness and increasing weakness.

She did not know that she had accomplished the seemingly impossible feat of crossing the lake until the skiff nosed gently into the soft sand and she was conscious that she was rowing against an immovable object. Dazed and almost fainting from exhaustion, she wondered what was holding her back. Then she heard a sharp command coming from somewhere in the predawn darkness.

"Halt or I'll fire!"

She stopped struggling and leaned over the oars, scarcely conscious. Someone else joined the sentry on guard.

"That must be Jim with the supplies," he said. Then he called out, "Is that you, Jim? Answer or I'll fire!"

She raised her head wearily and spoke in a voice that they could scarcely hear.

"I've brought the supplies."

"It's a woman!" they cried and ran to her.

The dawn gave them a faint light and they saw her slumped over the oars. They helped her from the skiff, while one of them called out that the supplies had come at last. Men came running from the camp and gathered around.

"I can't walk," Diana moaned. "I've been shot."

They saw the crude bandage on her leg, so one of them took her in his arms and went toward the camp. They got the reticule with its precious contents from the skiff and they took her to the tent where the sick soldiers lay.

Now that she had at last reached the end of her journey, Diana gave way to exhaustion and sank into oblivion. The soldier who was acting as doctor came and examined the wound.

"That bullet will have to be removed," he remarked. "I just can't believe that she made it across. But she's probably saved the lives of a lot of us here."

He cleaned the wound and applied a clean dressing, then he left her to rest and recover while he administered the drugs to those who needed them most. While he was making his rounds, Ralph heard him telling the others about Diana's unbelievable feat. Then he came to Ralph. Ralph was still weak and shaken with malaria, but the fever had subsided for the present.

"I heard you say that a girl brought the drugs over," he told the soldier.

"Yes, and we can thank you for sending that note. It got the supplies over to us. I suppose Jim got caught. The young lady is wounded. Shot in the leg."

Ralph's heart seemed to stop beating.

"Where is she?" he asked.

"Over there in the corner. But you stay put. You're in no condition to be up and around."

Ralph ignored him and when he had left, he staggered over to where Diana lay. He stared at her in surprise, but she was asleep, so he went back to his own cot and lay there waiting for her to waken.

The sun was high before Diana opened her eyes. Her leg was throbbing painfully and she was burning with fever, but she was rested, so she sat up and looked about her. Then she remembered where she was. She had made it! Now perhaps she would be free from that haunting reproach about William's death. She had helped save the lives of these men. Perhaps that would atone for the death she had been responsible for.

She was hungry and she was glad when she saw a young woman coming in with a tray containing bowls of cereal. This girl was a volunteer who had been helping nurse the sick ever since the soldiers had arrived. Others living nearby had helped in other ways with food that they had brought from their gardens. Medicine had been the one thing they could not supply. She came to Diana and set the bowl before her.

"These men will never forget what you have done for them," she said. "You risked your life to save them and they'll thank you as long as they live."

"It was the least I could do," Diana told her.

When she had finished and the others had been served, she saw Ralph coming from the other end of the tent. She greeted him with a smile. Perhaps she could make him happy when this war was over. The old coquettish spirit was still there in spite of pain and illness and all that she had suffered.

"Ralph!" she exclaimed. "I'm so glad to see that you are better. I was hoping that the medicine would get here in time to help you."

"It did. It will help all of us and we'll never cease to thank you, but why did you do it? What happened to Jim?"

"I don't know. He didn't come and the Yankees were about to get the skiff, so I jumped in and brought it myself." She gave him an ardent look and added softly, "I got your note, Ralph dear. After what you told me in that note, what else could I do but bring the supplies, even at the risk of my life? I'm so glad you still love me."

He stared at her blankly for a moment, surprised at her words, then as he began to understand, he blurted out, "But the note was for Angela. I sent it to her."

The smile faded from her lips and she stared at him aghast.

"Angela," she repeated. "You mean that you're in love with her?"

He nodded. "Didn't she tell you? I hope to marry her if I ever live to get home again when this war is over."

She sank back upon the cot and closed her eyes to keep him from seeing what might be revealed there. She forced a smile as she lay there, so that he might not know how humiliated she was, how angry with him and with Angela for keeping this from her. She blamed Angela in this hour of her humiliation for having placed her in this situation. If she had known the truth when that note came, she would be at home now instead of suffering here in this miserable tent, in danger and in pain. Fury possessed her, but she could not afford to have Ralph see how she felt.

"I'm sorry if you misunderstood," Ralph was saying apologetically. He felt terribly embarrassed, for he realized that perhaps she had done this brave thing because she thought he loved her.

For a while she did not answer, but lay there fighting to

gain control of her emotions, then she opened her eyes and smiled again.

"I hope that you and Angela will be very happy. The little rascal never told me." Her voice was warm and friendly but within she was seething with anger and embarrassment. "Just be thankful that I got the note instead of her, for she never could have made that trip. Now please leave me. I'm very tired and I must rest."

He left her feeling guilty, though he knew that he had done nothing wrong.

Diana tried to be thankful that she had made this terrible mistake and that she had been able to accomplish that dangerous mission, but in her heart there was no such feeling, only anger and bitterness and a sense of frustration. She had followed a mirage and it might mean her death, for the fever raged higher and she knew the danger of infection from that bullet.

21

AT THE WILBORN HOME there was consternation. Diana's horse had returned home riderless. Roger discovered the horse standing at the gate. He questioned the stable boy and learned that Diana had had the horse saddled several hours previous. They were distracted and did not know what to do. Alicia was sure that Diana had met with some accident and might be lying dead somewhere, but they didn't know where to start looking. Finally Angela went to Diana's room to see if she could find anything that might give them some clue as to where she might have been going for a ride. She found the note that Diana had left on her dressing table.

"Don't be frightened when my horse comes home without me," she read. "And don't look for me or raise any alarm. The less you know about where I am, the better it will be for all of us. I'll get back home as soon as I can. I may have to walk, so don't be afraid, if I don't get back for some time."

That was all. Angela took the note to her father and he read it with a grave face.

"I wonder what she's up to now," he remarked when he had finished reading it. "We'd better do what she says. Don't mention this to anyone. I suppose she knows what she's doing. I hope so," he added with a sigh.

There was nothing to do but wait and hope and pray that she would return safely before long.

Across the lake where Diana was, the soldier who had examined her wound was standing beside her cot talking to her.

"That bullet will have to be extracted," he told her. "I'm no surgeon, but I have taken out enough bullets to do it fairly well. Thanks to you I have a sharp scalpel that will help me to do it less painfully than with a pocket knife. I've even dug them out with a kitchen knife. The longer that bullet stays in the worse it will be for you."

Diana shuddered but she tried to speak bravely.

"Do what you think best," she told him. "I've got to get back home as soon as I can."

"We'll talk about that later," he told her, then he prepared to remove the bullet.

The bullet was lodged against the bone and had shattered it slightly. He feared that infection had already set in and that the consequences might be grave. He had seen men lose their limbs from a similar injury. He knew that she would have to get back to where she could receive the proper care, though how this could be arranged he had no idea.

She fainted from the pain while he was extracting the bullet and he was glad of that, for before she recovered consciousness the deed was done and the wound was carefully bandaged. Then he discussed the problem of getting her back to town where she could receive the medical aid she needed. Ralph and several others were called into consultation. Finally the young woman who was acting as nurse offered a suggestion which they decided to act upon.

About half way to town, on the Manchac road, there was a fisherman's hut. This fisherman had a pass through the lines to take fish to the market. The girl suggested that they should take Diana there and let the fisherman take her to the city in his cart. She would be allowed to pass through the lines since she was so ill and was a civilian. There was the risk of her identity being discovered and consequent questions asked which might lead to trouble for her, but there seemed no other way, so they decided to try this plan.

Diana was anxious to try it for she was impatient to get home. She knew that her family would be worried about her. The pain in her leg was spreading and getting worse and her fever was raging still higher.

Two farmers who lived nearby agreed to take her to the fisherman's shack. One of them knew the fellow and he was sure that everything could be arranged with him to take Diana to the city.

They were not mistaken, for the fisherman was a loyal Confederate and he agreed to take her home. He was sure that he could pass the guards and go through the lines with her. Diana was made as comfortable as possible in his shack and waited as patiently as she could until time for him to drive to the city the next morning with his load of fish which he had seined that morning at break of day.

When he reached the sentry posted at the end of the road on the outskirts of the city and explained why he was taking her to the city, and when the soldier saw how ill the girl was, he searched the cart thoroughly, then let them pass. Diana was scarcely conscious and did not know where she was or what was going on when the fisherman finally stopped at her home and rang the bell. Roger came to the door and when he saw Diana's condition, he called Alicia and the servants who helped him carry Diana to her room. One of the servants was sent to summon the doctor at once.

When the doctor came and examined Diana's wound and took her temperature, he shook his head gravely. Diana was now delirious and could not tell them what had happened.

Days passed while the fever raged and the infection persisted, until the doctor feared that if she lived, she would lose her leg. During this time she murmured broken phrases which puzzled them and which brought terror to Angela. Diana murmured snatches of her flight across the lake and of her meeting with Ralph. The mention of Ralph's name brought tears to Angela's eyes when she got a brief mention of him being ill in a tent, but she could not make sense out of Diana's snatches of what had happened.

Finally, after they had almost given up hope, consciousness returned and Diana saw her family around her. At first she thought she must still be having those dreams that she had had for so long, but as she saw them smiling down at her, she knew that she was not dreaming, but that she was safe at home at last.

She was able to tell them all that had happened. When she told them about the note and the mistake she had made by thinking it was for her, her eyes rested upon Angela and the girl felt that Diana was angry with her.

Diana surprised her by saying more gently than Angela had ever heard her speak, "I'm glad that I got the note and made the mistake. If you had gotten it, you never could have made it across the lake and I would never have had the chance to undo the wrong I did to William, if what I did can atone for that wrong."

Angela knelt by the bed and put her arm around her sister.

"Diana, darling, I pray that you will be happy with the one you love when this war is over," she whispered.

"The one I love?" Diana echoed. "I don't know who that could be."

"You know, even though you would never admit it," Angela told her. "I shall pray that God will send him back to you."

For a few days after that it seemed that Diana was growing steadily worse until her life was despaired of. One day while Angela sat by the bed as she slept, Diana opened her eyes and smiled at her sister.

"I've been such a hateful person," she remarked. "How could any of you love me?"

"We don't know, we just do," Angela answered with a tremulous smile.

She was sure that Diana must be dying or she would never talk like this.

"Would you send Mammy to me?" Diana asked weakly. "I want to talk to her and I want her to talk to me. Tell her that I'm willing to listen to what she has tried to tell me time and time again in the past."

Angela flew to Mammy's room with the news that gave her such a thrill, even while it brought the fear of death that seemed so near. Mammy Sue had been a faithful nurse during Diana's illness, sitting beside her all through the night while the others slept. Alicia was not willing to trust anyone else. Mammy Sue was sleeping, resting for the night's duties, but she got up at once when Angela came in and wakened her, telling her the good news.

Diana greeted her with a faint smile.

"I want you to talk to me, Mammy, like you used to do when I was a little girl. I have had my lesson now and at last I'm willing to listen."

Mammy Sue sat down beside the bed as Angela went to her room and prayed while the two were talking.

"What you want me to talk about, chile?" Mammy asked.

"You know. About my soul. You've tried and tried to persuade me to listen but I didn't want to. I was having such a good time that I didn't want to hear about God or my need of taking Christ as my Saviour. Now I see after all this time, that my life has been wasted. The good times are gone and I have nothing left. I'm going to die, Mammy." She caught her breath with a little sob. "I wonder if God will forgive me when I've refused to listen to Him all these years."

"Co'se de Lawd'll fo'give you, honey, but you'se got to ask Him and you'se got to be sorry fo' puttin' Him off all dis time."

"I am sorry," Diana sighed. "I've been such a willful, headstrong little fool." She turned appealing eyes to the old

Negro. "Mammy, do you think God will forgive me for what I did to William? I can never have any peace in my heart, if I should live, if He doesn't."

"Sho' He will, but you got to ask Him. He done promised to fo'give all our sins, 'cause Jesus shed His blood fo' 'm on de Cross. But we got to ask Him and we got to want Him to come into our hearts and give us eternal life. You know dat, chile, so what's de use o' my tellin' you all oveh again?"

"I just wanted to hear it again." Tears welled up in her eyes and ran down her pale cheek. "I heard the doctor tell Mother that if I did get well, I'd probably lose my leg. I'd rather die than lose my leg. But I don't want to die without taking Christ as my Saviour."

"You ain't gonna die and you ain't gonna lose dat leg," Mammy asserted confidently. "De Lawd done settled dat wid me. He say you gwine get well and you gwine be happier dan you done eveh been, cause you'll have peace in yo' hea't."

Diana smiled feebly. "What makes you so sure?"

"What you think I'se been doin' all dese nights when I was watchin' oveh you? I been prayin' fo' yo' soul and fo' dat leg and fo' you to get well and de Lawd just somehow tole me dat eve'thing wus gwine turn out all right and my prayers wus gwine be answered."

"Pray with me, Mammy, won't you please?" Diana asked.

"Co'se I will, honey chile, but you got to pray too for yo' own self."

"I will. Oh, I will!" Diana cried.

Mammy Sue knelt by the bed and prayed earnestly that Diana might receive the precious gift of salvation and then Diana prayed while the tears flowed, that God would forgive her and save her soul. Then Mammy rose from her knees and bent down and kissed Diana upon her forehead. Diana threw her arms around the old woman's neck and held her while she murmured, "Thank you for what you've done for me. It's all right now. God has forgiven me. I know I shall have peace."

She smiled through her tears while Mammy, with tears in her own eyes, stood looking down at her and murmured words of praise and thanksgiving. Angela came in just then. She couldn't stay away any longer.

Mammy turned to her with a smile and said, "De Lawd had to whip her down, but she done come through at last. Dis gwine be her second birthday."

When the doctor came again he found his patient so much improved that he had hopes that she would recover. He still hoped that she would not have to lose her leg. Her recovery was slow, but she gained strength gradually until she could stand up and walk a few steps. She was very weak and the wound in her leg still pained her. When she was stronger and able to walk a little longer, she limped badly. The doctor told her that she would not lose that leg as he had feared, but that she would always have that limp, for the injury had impaired the knee joint.

She smiled bravely, though the news was a shock.

"I'm thankful that I'm still alive and that I didn't have to lose my leg. A little limp won't matter too much. I'll never be able to dance again, but then I'll never want to dance, now that I've taken Christ as my Saviour. I shall be happier than I've ever been before because I have peace in my heart."

The doctor was a Christian and he understood and shared her new found joy.

22

THE WAR CONTINUED TO ITS disastrous end for the South. Vicksburg finally surrendered in July, 1863, after the long and bitter siege, and the whole Mississippi Valley was open to the Union forces. Blow after blow came to the Confederacy: the death of General Jonathan "Stonewall" Jackson, shot by mistake by one of his own men after the victory at Chancellorsville, the disastrous defeat at Gettysburg following a carnage of slaughter on both sides, Sherman's march to the sea through Georgia, leaving death and destruction in his wake.

At last came the meeting of Lee and Grant at Appomatox Court House when Lee surrendered his ragged army and handed his sword to the northern general. As they met each looked into the eyes of the other, Lee, the Southern gentleman and Christian soldier and Grant, the burly, masterful leader who had risen to become one of the great generals and an invincible enemy. Each recognized the greatness of the other.

As Grant looked at the tattered, starving remains of Lee's army, his heart softened with sympathy toward a valiant foe who would no longer be an enemy, for he was still a great American. He handed Lee his sword again. He could keep it. It was the symbol of one of the greatest military leaders of all time and he could not let him go in disgrace. Lee accepted the concession with dignity and appreciation, though there was the hint of tears in his eyes.

Grant proved his own greatness of heart by allowing Lee's men to keep their horses.

"You'll need them for ploughing," he told them.

And so a great general with a heart saddened by the memory of the useless slaughter of a useless war, returned to private life while the soldiers under him returned to their homes which had been devastated and to poverty such as they had never known and to years of struggle to recover what they had lost through the war.

* * * * *

It was summer again. Lilacs and roses and honeysuckle bloomed in profusion in the plantation garden, while their sweet perfume pervaded the air and was wafted by the gentle breeze to the porch where Diana sat. Dusk was creeping through the trees. It hushed the singing of the birds to a muted twittering as they sought their perches for the night.

The family had returned once more to the plantation. Alicia and the servants had been busy getting the house in order while Roger had been occupied going over the plantation which had been somewhat neglected during the war. There had been so little opportunity for the sale of sugar since their outlet had been blocked by the Union forces that the sugar mill had not been operating. Roger was anxious to get it going in the fall so that the meagre cane crop could be harvested and his much depleted fortune partially restored. This evening he and Alicia were in the living room playing a game of dominoes.

Angela was in the den with Ralph. They had announced their engagement and would be married in the fall. The wedding would be a quiet affair instead of the elaborate one which would have been possible if the war had not come.

Diana was very happy for Angela. Angela had matured during the war years. She was still full of fun and the desire to spread the joy of life to others, but she had outgrown her childish habit of teasing. She and Diana had grown very close and they were now inseparable. This was because Diana had changed. The old discontented, bitter spirit had disappeared and in its place there had come a gentleness that amazed everyone while they rejoiced over it. Even though she limped badly and, because of her lameness, had been denied many of the activities which she once enjoyed, she never complained. She was thoughtful of others instead of being self-centered and self-ish. She exhibited every evidence that she had truly been born again that day when she had prayed for forgiveness and had received the gift of salvation.

She felt rather lonely this evening. Her mother and father had each other, Angela and Ralph had each other and she was, in a sense, alone. Her host of admirers had not returned after the war had ended. One reason was that she had not encouraged them to come. There was not one of them that she cared for when she had pretended to while she was flirting with them. Then, also, though she did not complain, she felt her lameness keenly. She had lost the desire to charm men and to enslave them by the power of that charm and she felt that, because she was a cripple, she would never be attractive again to any man.

She was thinking of Keith. She thought of him often and wondered where he was, if he was still living and, if he was, if he would ever come back to his plantation. The plantation was almost as neglected as it was when he first came. Most of the slaves had left to seek their fortunes elsewhere, though some of the older ones who had grown to love him had remained to care for the place and to eke out a living until his return. She wondered what he would think of her, if he should ever see her again, now that she was a cripple. She wished that he could know that she had at last surrendered her stubborn will to the Lord. At least he would respect her if he knew that.

Presently she saw a horseman approaching the gate. He opened it and walked his horse to the hitching post. When he turned toward the steps she recognized him. He was very thin, almost emaciated, and there was a droop to his shoulders that had not been there before, but he was still as handsome as ever, even more handsome, she thought as her hungry eyes rested upon him.

He stood looking at her silently, gazing with rapt eyes upon her face so lovely in the dusk. She was thinner and more mature, but she seemed more beautiful than ever. The old defiant, cynical look had left her eyes. In its place there was a glow that seemed to spread over her face and told him in some subtle way that she had changed. He noticed that she limped badly as she rose and came toward him.

She stood waiting for him to speak, wondering why he was silent so long.

"Keith!" she murmured as he stood looking at her. "I can't believe it is really you."

"May I come in?" he asked diffidently.

"Of course!. Why do you have to ask that? Haven't you always been welcome here?"

As he mounted the steps she gave him her hand and he took it and held it in both of his.

"I was afraid you might think that I'm still your enemy."

"The war is over, Keith," she replied, "and there should be no more enemies among us. We are still Americans and you are still our friend, if that is what you want to be."

"That is what I want more than anything."

The look he gave her brought the blood rushing to her face and made her heart beat wildly. She led the way to the wide swing and they sat down together.

"I wondered if you would ever come back here," Diana said in the silence that fell between them.

"I came back as soon as I could get my discharge. I didn't know how the people around here would feel about me, but I had to get back and try to get the plantation going again."

"We didn't hear from you after General Banks came and we wondered why."

"We were under orders not to have any communication with the citizens except on business. Just before orders for my detachment to be sent north I was in the hospital and for a long time they thought I would die. When I was well enough, I was shipped off and was in the thick of battle until the war ended."

"What was the trouble when you were so ill?" she asked.

"I was shot. The bullet lodged so near my heart that they were afraid to try to remove it. It was not removed until after I had been sent north."

"How did it happen?" she asked. "Was it an accident?"

He smiled. "I'm sure that it was an accidental hit, one of those freak accidents, though the shot was meant to kill and was no accident. And it almost did what the one who fired it hoped it would. I was on duty with my men, guarding the lake front from possible runners trying to get medical supplies across to the Confederates. We shot at someone getting into a skiff. One of the soldiers thought it was a woman but no woman could shoot like that. He fired back while I was at close range, just after I had fired at him and that shot got me."

She stared at him with wide eyes and uttered a smothered exclamation.

"It's too impossible! It just can't be real!" she cried.

"What can't be real?" he asked. "That shot was very real, even though it was uncanny in the dusk when sight must have been bad. It was a hit in a thousand and the fellow who fired it got away clean, even though I had aimed at him before he shot at me."

She spoke slowly and with difficulty, still unable to believe such a strange coincidence.

"I was the one who fired that shot, Keith. And to think that I almost killed you! How I thank God that I didn't!"

"You!" he cried. "That's impossible. What were you doing out there?"

"It's a long story, Keith, and I'll give you the details some other time, but you didn't miss me, Keith. I was shot in the leg by someone whom I shot at just after he had fired. It must have been you. That's why it seems so unbelievable."

"Is that what made you limp?" he asked.

"Yes. Infection set in and they thought I would die, but the Lord not only saved my life, He saved my soul. While I was lying there helpless and feeling terribly despondent, I had time to think of my life and how rebellious I had been. Mammy Sue came and prayed with me and the Lord forgave me and saved me. I'm grateful for that wound, even though I shall always be a cripple, for if that had not happened, I might never have yielded my will to the Lord."

"Then you don't hate me?" he asked with a tender smile.

"The Bible tells us to love our enemies, so how could I hate you?"

The smile that accompanied the words reminded him of Angela when they were exchanging repartee.

"Oh Diana!" he exclaimed in a hushed voice, "I've thought of you a thousand times each day and longed for a sight of you, even though you acted as if you hated me. I wanted you even though I knew that I should not, since you were not a Christian. I love you, my darling, with all the love of my heart. Can you ever learn to love me? Tell me that you'll try." He took her hand and drew her closer and she didn't pull away. "I don't want just what the Bible says," he remarked whimsically. "I want you to say what you really feel in your heart."

"What I really feel in my heart is what I believe I have felt all along," she told him. "I think I've loved you almost from that first morning when my horse threw me and I was so angry and so impolite with you. I felt, though, that you disapproved of me and when you told me that even though you loved me you would never marry me, I tried to make myself believe that I hated you. But I know now that I never did. I do love you, Keith, not only because the Bible tells me to, but because I want to. I love you with all my heart."

He took her in his arms and her lips met his, this time in glad surrender.

"How good the Lord is to bring us together again," Keith murmured. "We shall spend our lives together trying to serve Him."

"You haven't asked me if I would spend my life with you," she reminded him. "You said once you'd never ask me to marry you. And you haven't. Have you changed your mind?"

He laughed a low, happy laugh as he held her close.

"That's a woman's privilege, but I claim it now. Mistress Wilborn, will you do me the honor to become my wife?"

"I'll consider it, sir," she replied.

They both laughed happily, then Diana became serious.

"I shall always be a cripple, Keith. Will you want a cripple for a wife?"

"When I was the one who made a cripple of you? What a question!" he answered. "Even if you had lost that leg, I would still love you and still want you. Deep, abiding love can't be destroyed by physical handicaps. And my love is just that."

She sighed happily as she rested in the circle of his arms.

"Shall we go in and tell the others?" he suggested presently. "I want them to know."

"Yes, let's. I shall tell them that the last rebel has surrendered."

Together they went into the house with his arm around her and her lovely face alight with a joy she thought she would never know.